JUSTIFIED

Aurora Rose Reynolds

Copyright © 2014 Crystal Aurora Rose Reynolds Print Edition
Print Edition

Designs Formatted by BB eBooks

All rights reserved. No part of this book may be reproduced or transmitted in any form or by any means, electronic or mechanical, including photocopying, recording, or by any information storage and retrieval system, without permission in writing.

This is a work of fiction. Names, characters, places and incidents are the product of the author's imagination or are used factiously, and any resemblance to any actual persons or living or dead, events or locals are entirely coincidental.

The author acknowledges the trademark status and trademark owners of various products referenced in this work of fiction, which have been used without permission. The publication/ Use of these trademarks is not authorized, associated with, or sponsored by the trademark owner.

All rights reserved.

TABLE OF CONTENTS

Chapter 1	1
Chapter 2	13
Chapter 3	31
Chapter 4	43
Chapter 5	55
Chapter 6	63
Chapter 7	72
Chapter 8	82
Epilogue	92
Other books by this Author	95
About The Author	96
Acknowledgment	98

DEDICATION

To my Roses, thank you for all your encouragement.

CHAPTER 1

"Tilt that pussy." I pound into her as my hand slaps down on her ass hard. Seeing my handprint appear on her smooth, pale skin makes me grunt out in satisfaction.

"Fuck me harder."

"Shut your mouth," I growl, wrapping my hand around her throat, pulling her up, and impaling her on my cock. "You know the rules." I bite down on her earlobe, causing her to whimper. "You don't talk when I'm fucking you unless I tell you to."

She nods, and I push her back down. My hand slides up her back to her neck, pressing her face deeper into the mattress.

I pound into her harder until I feel her walls clamping down on me. Then I thrust into her ruthlessly. Lifting my leg up on the bed, I change the angle. She's a tiny little thing, but I know she can take me. She always takes whatever I give her. I pull her hips up, slowing my rhythm, enjoying the feel of my cock dragging along her walls. She's so wet that, every time my cock slides out, it's shiny with her come. I pull out of her and flip us so she's on top.

"Ride me," I command, lifting my hips, filling her once more.

Her body starts bouncing up and down, her tits dancing in my face. Her large, natural Ds should look awkward on her tiny frame, but they go with her fat ass. I love everything about this woman. The visual in front of me has me getting close. I grab her hips, holding her in place as I fuck up into her. Then I come hard, long jets of seed filling her tight little pussy.

"I love you," she says quietly.

I tug her down on top of me, kissing the top of her head. I had no idea when I met Chloe that she was going to change my life, but slowly, this waif of woman has burrowed under my skin.

"Love you too, Beautiful." I press another kiss to the top of her head. And my mind drifts back to the past…

I was so fucking jaded when I found out that my ex-wife—the fucking bitch—was having an affair. Then I found Chloe by accident, and seeing her for the first time shifted something inside me. I had been on my cell phone and looked up to tell my client my cross street when my eyes landed on her through the bakery window. Without even thinking, I went across the street, and the moment I stepped inside the bakery, she turned towards the door and our eyes connected.

I have never believed in love at first sight or any of that other bullshit, but that moment was like a kick to the gut.

I walked to the counter and realized that my client was still on the phone, so I told him I would call him back and hung up. When she stepped towards me, the scent of lavender and vanilla filled my nose and the urge to grab her and bury my face in the crook of her neck was so strong that it was almost painful. Our gaze stayed connected until she was close enough to touch. Then the moment was broken when an old man came around the corner and told her that he would take care of me. I shook myself out of my daze, paid for a cup of coffee that would end up in the trash, and left the bakery in a rush. I wasn't fond of the feelings I was having. I'd had plenty of women, but seeing her was something different.

I wanted to possess her.

I needed to own her.

I fought myself on going back to her but settled on having my driver wait outside the bakery for hours so I could watch her through the window. On days when men would be inside with her, talking to her, making her laugh, I had to stop myself from going inside and taking her away with me.

She was mine.

She just didn't know it.

The first time I spoke to her in person, she smiled at me. I knew she was innocent the moment I had spoken to her—her head ducked, her face turned pink, and that look sealed her fate.

She would be mine.

Only mine.

I waited for her that night across the street. I watched her lock up before walking across the road and meeting her on the sidewalk.

"How are you getting home?" I asked her.

Her head came up, her big, brown eyes met mine, and the surprise I saw filled me with another kind of satisfaction.

"I...I walk," she stuttered quietly.

"I'll walk you," I told her, not giving her a choice. My woman wouldn't be out at night alone.

I don't give a fuck what people say about women's rights and all that other bullshit. I'd let my ex do whatever the fuck she wanted, and look where the fuck that had gotten me. No more—my woman would be at home, barefoot and pregnant until she could no longer safely bear my children.

"I always walk myself," she said softly, biting her bottom lip. Making me crave to do the same.

"Not anymore," I stated, holding out my hand for her.

She looked at it for a few seconds before placing her small hand in mine. The feeling of her fragileness in my grasp was almost too much. My gut clenched and I fought myself not to carry her over to my car, where I could take her home and hide her away, keeping her only to myself. I mentally talked myself down.

I needed her to trust me.

I needed her addicted to me.

Then she would be mine, and I would never have to let her go again.

"Who are you?" she asked, looking up at me with wide, innocent eyes.

I looked her over. The top of her head barely came up to the middle of my chest. Her hair was dark brown with reddish highlights, and it reached the middle of her back. Her skin was the color of cream mixed with honey. I could picture my marks all over her beautiful skin. Her eyes were dark brown with long lashes that I could tell were natural. She didn't wear makeup; she didn't need it. She was naturally beautiful.

"Nolan," I told her.

Her eyes looked me over, and I knew what she saw: black hair, darker skin that's natural from my Spanish-American heritage, and dark-brown eyes surrounded by dark lashes. I'd been told a time or two that I'm good-looking. I wore my age of thirty-four well. And I'd never had an issue getting a woman.

My private investigator had informed me that Chloe had just turned twenty-two. I couldn't give a fuck about our age difference. My mind was telling me that the younger she was, the more likely I would be able to train her into being exactly what I wanted. He'd also done some digging into her past and hadn't been able to find out about any previous relationships. This suited me just fine. I didn't even want to think about someone other than me touching her…ever.

We walked the rest of the way to her apartment in silence. I didn't like the area she was living in, but I would have to wait to resolve that issue. I just needed to figure out how to force her out of her current residence and into mine.

"Thank you for walking me," *she said, trying to pull her hand from mine.*

I didn't let up. I wasn't able to let go. Her breathing picked up slightly, causing her breasts to press tighter against her top. Without thinking, I lowered my mouth over hers, taking her in a deep kiss, pushing my tongue between her lips. I could tell she was unsure; she didn't know that what she was doing would only egg me on.

I wanted to consume her.

I wanted to brand her.

The need to own her, possess her, was almost crippling.

I pulled my mouth from hers; my lips traveled down her jaw. Her body had melted into mine, so I took the opportunity to suck the skin of her neck in deep pulls that I knew would mark her for anyone to see. I needed to know that, tomorrow, when she went to work, I was going with her. I had a big case I was working on and couldn't sit outside the bakery like I normally would, so she would be on her own, my mark a warning against any man who tried to get to close to her.

"I'll see you tomorrow, Beautiful." *I kissed her neck and then her mouth again.*

Her eyes were hazy, and I knew she didn't understand what she was feeling. Her body was in control right now. I walked her into her apartment and made sure she was locked in for the night. After I knew she was safely tucked away, I went back to my limo.

"Sir," *Ricket said, opening the back door.*

I nodded, getting into the car without saying a word. Once we were on our way, I called one of my men and put him on her building for the night, telling him to report to me after he followed her to work in the morning. I was a little anxious to get back to her, but I knew I had to play my cards right.

I couldn't rush this no matter what my inner beast was telling me to do.

By the time I pulled up in front of my building across town, I was restless. So instead of going to bed, I went down to the gym. Normally when I felt like this, I would fuck until I passed out, but I couldn't do that. Chloe was the only woman I wanted. I hit the treadmill hard, running until my legs felt weak, and then I went to the weights. I worked out until my body was exhausted.

"Mr. Nolan."

I lifted my head at the sound of my assistant's voice. Maxine had been with me for the last four years. I'd shut her down the first couple of times she had given me a look that said she wanted more than I would give her. She had calmed down, but seeing the appreciation in her eyes had me gritting my teeth.

"What do you need, Maxine?"

"I wanted to remind you about your meeting in the morning, and I also wanted to see if you needed to go over the notes for the case tomorrow."

"Thank you, and no. You're free for the rest of the night," I told her, going back to doing crunches. I could feel her watching me, but I ignored her. I wasn't in the mood to deal with anyone.

"See you tomorrow, sir," she said, and I heard the door close as she left the gym.

I finished working out before jogging upstairs and getting into the shower. My cock had been rock hard since the first time I'd seen Chloe. Just like my mind, my body had been taken over by her. I wrapped my hand around my length and pumped twice. Then I thought about how I'd be wasting my come by shooting it down the drain when I could fill Chloe's womb with it and released myself.

I was in unchartered territory with her. When I had been married right out of law school, I'd thought I was doing the right thing. My wife, Lynda, was my father's best friend's daughter. I respected her and thought, at the time, that I loved her. She was beautiful and interesting, and she had a good head on her shoulders. We were married for six years when I told her I wanted to have a child with her. When she agreed, we did the normal things while planning for a baby.

When it didn't happen after a year, I decided that we should talk to a specialist about it. I had no idea that my wife had gotten her tubes tied until I showed up to an appointment she hadn't expected to see me at. When the doctor let it slip what she had done shortly after we'd decided to have a child, during a time when she was supposed to have been at a conference for a week, I left the office in a rage. I couldn't believe she had gone behind my back and done something so deceiving. That's when I decided to find out what else I didn't know about the woman I married.

The night the investigator gave me the case file on my wife was one of the most eye-opening experiences of my life. I hadn't known that women could lead double lives—at least not the kind of double life she was leading. Not only had she gotten her tubes tied, but she had also been in a long-term relationship with another man for most of our marriage. I'd never once let my eyes wander from her. I'd had plenty of opportunities to take on a mistress or two, but when I'd vowed to be faithful, I had taken it seriously.

The night I found out who I really had in my bed, I went home and handed her the file, and without a word, she went to the bedroom and began to pack.

Angry would not be an accurate representation of the emotion I was feeling. I could have killed her. I actually thought about killing her. Then I thought about the way I could really hurt her. Her father had passed away a few years before, leaving her alone since her mother was in a special hospital in upstate New York. My dear wife was on her own.

I was her only source of income since she didn't work. She was a typical Upper East Side wife. Her boyfriend was a banker who lived in an apartment in the Bronx. His net income was around sixty thousand a year. Her lifestyle would take a drastic change, and she would never get shit from me. I had enough evidence against her that I didn't need to worry about her. Even the best divorce attorney in the world wouldn't have been able to force me to give her one penny.

It took six months to get my divorce finalized. Lynda tried to fight me, but in the end, she wasn't able to get one red dime and her boyfriend dumped her. I learned later that he'd had no idea she was married and hadn't taken kindly to her using him to cheat on another man...

A knock on the door brings me out of my thoughts about the past, and I'm just about to yell for them to go away when the door is swung open and Maxine walks in without even waiting for me to reply.

"Get the fuck out!" I roar, causing Chloe, who had fallen asleep on top of me, to jump in her sleep. I quickly pull the covers over us. I don't give a fuck about me, but I don't want anyone—even a woman—to see Chloe like she is now.

"Sorry," I hear whispered as the door quickly closes.

"What's wrong?" Chloe mumbles sleepy, raising her head to look at me.

"Nothing. Go back to sleep, love," I say quietly, kissing her forehead.

She sighs and closes her eyes, laying her head back down. Once I hear her breath even out, I slide out from under her and make sure she's covered before pulling on a pair of pajama pants, grabbing my cell phone, and heading for the main living room.

"What did you need, Maxine?" I ask as soon as my assistant answers the phone.

"Sorry, sir. I thought you would want to know your conference call with Japan got canceled. I tried phoning you, but it went straight to voicemail."

"Maxine, I don't care if the world outside my bedroom door is imploding upon itself. When that door is closed, you do not ever open it," I growl into the phone.

"I'm sorry. I didn't know she was there," she says, but even in her tone, I can hear bitterness.

I take a deep breath and let it out slowly. "Maxine, I expect the keys you have for my loft to be returned tomorrow. You will no longer be allowed into the building. I understand you have a job to do, but you will no longer have the access you had before."

"Sir!" she gasps, and I shake my head, looking out at the city below me.

"This isn't the first time you've overstepped your bounds, but this will be the last," I tell her firmly.

"I apologized," she whispers.

"And that is the only reason you still have a job," I state before hanging up the phone.

I press my forehead to the glass and look out at the street below. Then I feel a small hand on my back slide around to my chest as Chloe's cheek presses into my skin.

"Are you okay?" she whispers as I cover her small hand with mine before turning around and looking down at her.

She's wearing the white dress shirt I had on earlier in the evening—only one button is in place, holding it together. Her hair is down around her shoulders, and her face is clean of any makeup. Just looking at her makes my breath catch in my throat.

"Better now," I grunt out as my fingers slide into the open top of the shirt and down around her nipple.

A small whimper leaves her mouth as her eyes slide closed.

"My beautiful angel," I whisper, dropping my mouth to hers, forcing my tongue between her lips.

When her small hand falls against my chest, I drop my hands to the back of her legs and pick her up, lifting her and wrapping her thighs around my waist. I turn and press her back to the window, my hips firmly between her legs, giving me leverage to use my hands to remove my shirt from her.

She cries out from the cold of the glass, and goose bumps breakout over her skin. Her nails tear against the skin of my shoulders as I lift her higher, pulling her breast into my mouth. I feel pre-cum pearl at the head of my cock, and the slick heat of her arousal between her legs rubs against my lower stomach. I want to lift her up and wrap her legs around my face while burying my tongue deep inside her. The fact that she was innocent before me only makes fucking her and eating her that much more intoxicating. Knowing that the only come to have ever filled her pussy is mine is extraordinary.

"I can feel your juices all over my stomach. Do you want me to eat you, Beautiful? Or do you want my cock deep inside your soaking-wet pussy?" I ask her as her fingers dig into my hair.

My brain is racing. One part of me wants to consume her, and the other part of me wants to lower my pants and slide inside her. The side of me that's been trying to breed her wins out, so I use one hand to push down the front of my pants. Then I wrap my hand around my girth while pulling her forward and down, filling her until the head of my cock bumps against her cervix.

I watch her eyes roll back and her head fall against the window behind her. I slowly slide out then back in with deep, smooth, long strokes, enjoying every inch of her pussy rippling around me. She was made for me, her pussy built to be taken by me alone.

"Look at you…so fucking beautiful. Even with a view behind you that people pay millions for, you still outshine it." My eyes lower to our connection and I watch myself disappear inside her. "Men would kill to see what I see right now," I tell her on a grunt, pressing deeper inside her. "But you're mine. You belong to me and only me, and I will kill anyone who even tries to get too close to you, anyone who even imagines seeing you like I see you," I growl, the thought of another man even thinking of her making me want to kill.

She is my obsession.

Her hips begin to rotate and my head falls back. I know that, if I let her continue her movements, I will shoot off inside her before I'm ready. So I still her hips and pull her from the glass, walking to the couch that faces the fireplace and laying her along the back. After sliding out of her and kissing her before nibbling down her body, I pause over her pussy, where I let out a long breath. Lying like this, she's stuck; she can't move or she will fall over the back or onto the couch.

"Stay still so you don't fall," I tell her and kiss her above her pubic bone before licking up her center, circling her clit, and then pulling it into my mouth between my lips. Her back arches and the couch wobbles as I fill her with two fingers. "Careful," I hiss against her, fucking her slowly with my fingers as I suck on her pussy, letting her juices flow into my mouth.

Once I feel her little pussy start to convulse around my fingers,

I lift my face, running my tongue around her belly button before sucking on each of her nipples. Then I kiss up her neck to her mouth, where she sucks on my tongue and lips, taking her taste off my mouth.

I hold her hips firmly as I enter her again; my cock is so hard that I feel my pulse beating through it. Her body slides with each thrust and her head slips over the side of the couch, her back bent, her hands on the cushion of the couch near her head. While her tits are bouncing with each thrust, her legs wrap around me as she is made completely helpless in this position.

I fuck into her, sliding my thumb over her clit in quick circles. She screams out as her pussy strangles my cock. The feeling of her walls clamping down on me has me standing on my tiptoes and pounding harder until my balls draw up and I come deep inside her. Then I take a deep breath, put my hands under her arms, and lift her slight weight up while she's still impaled on me. Her body slumps into mine as I carry her around to the front of the couch and sit with her on my lap.

My chest is moving rapidly along with hers. I can feel her heart beating hard against my own as I look down at her, and I move her hair off her face, seeing that her eyes are still closed. Leaning my head back, I say a prayer of thanks that she was given to me.

CHAPTER 2

"DO YOU WANT to explain to me why Mr. Yakamora called to tell me you missed your conference call this morning?"

I look up from the file I have been going over at my associate, Wesly, one of the five men who own the law firm along with me, and my eyebrows pull together.

"The meeting was canceled," I state, sitting back in my chair.

"By whom?" he asks.

Since I never asked Maxine who called and canceled the meeting, I have no way of knowing that information until Maxine gets back to the office.

"I'm not sure. Maxine is the one who received the information." I sigh, rubbing between my eyes.

"Well, now Mr. Yakamora is demanding you go to Japan and meet in person. Normally, I would say fuck him, but this case would be over twelve million alone, and we can't risk losing that kind of profit right now."

"Fuck," I mutter, knowing he's right but pissed that I have to leave Chloe for any length of time.

"Sorry, man. I would handle this myself, but you know he only wants to deal with you."

"I'll get this figured out. Tell Charles to schedule the jet for a red-eye flight to Tokyo," I tell him as I gather my documents and briefcase. "I need to head home to pack. I'll call you once I reach Japan."

"We'll talk then. Good luck, man," he says, patting my back.

I pull my phone out of my pocket and call Ricket to tell him to meet me out front. As soon as I exit the building, my limo is idling at the curb and Ricket is standing on the sidewalk, holding the door open.

"Where to, sir?"

"Chloe. Then home. I'll be leaving for Japan tonight," I tell him, anxious about being away from her. "I'll take a car service to the airport so you can make sure Chloe gets home safely. Also, put Bernard on her until I get home," I tell Ricket, loosening my tie.

"Yes, sir," he says, pulling away from the curb.

When we arrive at the bakery, I step out and see Chloe through the glass window, sitting at a small table in the front of the store. She's talking to a woman who looks familiar, but I can't place where I know her from. When I walk into the bakery, Chloe's eyes come to me and her face lights up. I watch as she says something to the woman before walking directly to me.

"Hey, you," she whispers.

I lower my face and kiss her while wrapping my hand around the back of her neck so I can keep her anchored to me. "Angel," I say against her mouth, standing up to my full height. "Do you have a moment?"

"Um, sure," she says as her eyebrows draw together. "Just let me tell Lee we're going to be outside."

I nod, release her from my hold, and watch as she walks away to the back of the bakery. When she comes back, I open the door for her and step out onto the busy sidewalk, taking her hand and walking her to the back of the limo. Once I have her seated in my lap, I turn her face towards me and look at her for a moment.

"What's going on?" she asks, searching my face.

"I'm leaving for Japan tonight. I should be home Monday if everything goes as planned."

"Oh," she mutters, her shoulders slumping forward.

Even though she refuses to move into my loft, she has been there every night. We haven't been apart for more than a few hours since the first time I took her. I want her with me, but she continues to say that she doesn't feel comfortable living with me without us having a more solid footing in our relationship. What the hell that means, I have no fucking clue. All the women I have met in the past would have jumped at the opportunity to have a man take care of them, but my beautiful angel is not like all women, I suppose.

"It's Wednesday," she says as her fingers wrap into the collar of my suit jacket.

"I'll be back before you know it. Ricket will be taking you to and from work while I'm gone, and Bernard will be looking after you."

"I'm not afraid of being alone. I'm just going to miss you," she says, placing her forehead against mine.

"Angel," I whisper, wrapping my fingers into her hair and pulling her mouth to mine. Once I have enough of her taste on my tongue, I release her and sit back. "You need to be good while I'm away. I need to know that you're safe," I say as my fingers dig into the skin of her waist. The thought of something happening to her when I'm not around is enough to make me crazy.

"I'll be working most of the time you're gone. Then I have some stupid bachelorette party to go to on Saturday, an—"

"What?" I growl, cutting her off.

"My friend, Bre—the girl I was talking to when you walked in? Well, she's getting married and invited me to her bachelorette party this weekend. Normally, I wouldn't go, but she keeps asking and I feel bad. I don't think she has many friends," she says softly, reading the look on my face.

I trust Chloe, but I do not trust anyone else with her. While saying that, I also know I can't exactly say no in this situation. So, like the lawyer I am, I immediately begin to formulate an argument that will lead to an outcome I can live with.

"Since I won't be here, and I know how things can happen when women get together, I need you to allow me to supply security while you're out with your friend," I state.

She pulls her bottom lip into her mouth and begins to nibble at it while searching my face. Regardless of whether or not she agrees to these terms, I will have my men on her twenty-four-seven while I'm away. The only difference will be that, in this situation, she will know they are there.

"I don't know how they will feel about having some scary-looking security hanging around," she says with a small smile.

"My men are professionals," I growl, kissing her neck, making her laugh.

"Where do you even find them, mobhenchmen.com?"

"Very funny, Angel." I chuckle and tuck some loose hair behind her ear. "I need to know you're safe," I repeat sternly.

"If they don't make it obvious they are there, then it's fine," she says, giving me exactly what I need, and I reward her with a kiss. "What time is your flight?" she asks, tucking her head under my chin.

"Late." I sigh, pulling her tighter against me. "I still need to head home to the condo so I can pack," I say quietly, enjoying the peace only she can bring me.

"I should probably get back into the shop," she whispers after a few minutes, sitting up, and as much as I don't want to let her go, I know I need to.

"Kiss me," I demand.

She does as she's told, her small tongue touching my bottom lip, making my cock, which was already at half-mast from having her on my lap, rise completely. I hate that I can't have her one more time before I must go out of town. I take over the kiss, sucking her tongue into my mouth and then nibbling on her lips before pulling away, kissing her gently one last time.

"Be safe on your trip. I love you," she says quietly, pressing her soft lips to mine once more.

"Love you, Angel," I tell her, sitting for a second longer, willing my erection to go down.

After moving her off my lap and opening the door to the limo, I get out, taking her hand in mine before walking her back across the street. Then I pull her into my arms one final time, breathing her in before opening the door to the bakery for her and watching her head inside. When I see her head towards the table where her friend is sitting, I take a moment to watch. The woman looks through the glass at me, and something about her triggers a memory I can't place. She smiles, but I don't return it, instead looking at Chloe, who waves. I lift my chin at her and head back across the street.

As soon as I'm seated inside the limo, I look at Ricket in the rearview mirror. "Call Bernard and tell him Chloe will be going out Saturday night and I want men on her while I'm out of town."

"Will do, sir." He nods.

"I also want to know how far along we are on getting her building condemned."

"They're still working on it, sir."

"Tell them if they can get it done before I get home, I will add another half a million."

"Will do, sir," Ricket says.

I know he will do anything I ask of him. He has been with me since I was a teen, and he's one of the few people I would trust with my life.

AFTER GOING HOME and packing, I make it to the airport and wait in the limo, sending Maxine a quick message about her fuck-up before calling Chloe and making sure she got home okay.

"Hey, Angel."

"Hey. Are you at the airport?" she asks.

I can hear the water turn on and the sound of her brushing her teeth. As crazy as it sounds, I'm pissed that I'm missing a small moment like that with her.

"Yes," I say, looking out the window at my jet. "Are you in for the night?"

"Are you saying your men didn't tell you I was home already?" she asks, and I can hear the smile in her voice.

"I like hearing it for myself," I state then let out a frustrated breath when my driver taps on the window. "Be good while I'm away. I will call you in the morning. Make sure you wait for Ricket to take you to work in the tomorrow."

"I will. Don't worry about me," she says reassuringly.

"I will always worry about you when I'm not around to see to your care myself," I tell her.

I hear her sharp inhalation of breath. She still has a hard time accepting that I want to take care of her, how much I love her and want what's best for her. I'm sure my psychologist would have a field day if he knew what kind of shit I am thinking when it comes to Chloe. My feelings for her go above and beyond the realm of normal and into the categories of slightly crazy, obsessed, and extreme possession. The one thing I can say though is that at least I can admit it to myself, and if I'm being completely honest, I don't give a fuck what anyone thinks about my feelings for her. She's mine and has been from the first moment I saw her.

"I'll call you in the morning, Angel."

"Okay," she says. I can hear her getting into bed, and I grit my teeth. "Night," she whispers.

"Night, Angel," I say, hanging up, grabbing my bag, and heading for the plane.

"I'M HAVING A hard time believing you want my business," Mr. Yakamora says, and it takes everything in me not to growl.

"I wouldn't be here if I didn't want your business," I remind him again. Since I showed up in Tokyo, I have been hearing the same thing over and over. "I explained what happened with our meeting, apologized, and flew out here. My associates and I have been working this case since the beginning. If you feel another firm can do a better job, be my guest, but let me tell you, no firm in the world has the reputation we have. We're known for winning cases, sir." I sit back in my chair and loosen my tie.

He looks me over and sighs. "There is a lot of money on the line. We need to know you are completely involved."

"I have proven to you and your company that you have me and my firm's devotion. At this point, I do not know how else to demonstrate to you we are the best choice for you if you think you can get better representation somewhere else," I say again.

Just as I'm about ready to say fuck it and walk, he turns to me, his eyes searching my face.

"How do you feel about sake?" he asks with a wide smile, changing the subject and catching me off guard.

"Fucking hate the shit," I tell him, and he immediately begins to laugh as he comes towards me to pat my arm.

"You just haven't had it in the right environment."

I LOOK AROUND the club Mr. Yakamora's men brought us to and sigh. When I was recently divorced—hell, even when I was married—I would have been happy to spend my business trip in a place like this. Great food, good company, and beautiful women at your beck and call. But as I sit here, all I can think about is Chloe. Tonight, she would be going to a bachelorette party, and I have to rely on other people to watch over her. I still can't kick the strange feeling about the woman who was at the bakery with Chloe. I have no idea where I know her from, but something about her is familiar.

"You're not enjoying yourself," Mr. Yakamora observes, sitting down in the chair next to me and loosening his tie.

"I have a lot on my mind."

"Who is she?" he asks, calling a girl over with a wave of his fingers. When she's within hearing distance, he asks her in Japanese for another bottle of sake then turns back towards me. "I know it's a woman because only a woman can make a man look like he is somewhere else. I grew up hearing from my parents and grandparents that, when you find the woman you were meant for, your souls are always together, regardless of space or time."

I let his words sink in and relax back into my chair.

"So tell me. Who is she?" he asks.

I feel my jaw grind. I do not talk about Chloe to anyone, and I do not enjoy feeling like I have to choose between my personal life and the respect I have for a client.

"Ahh," Mr. Yakamora says quietly, steepling his fingers in front of him. "All right." He snaps his fingers on his right hand, and the waitress who had been taking his order comes over, setting a bottle of sake on the table along with two glasses. "I propose a toast." He pours the alcohol into one glass, handing it to me before pouring his own and setting the bottle down. "To space and time and the women who transcend it," he says.

We hold our glasses towards each other before taking a drink.

"Yes," I sleepily mumble into the phone after I finally get it to my ear.

"Sir, Chloe is in the hospital," Ricket says, and I sit up.

"What do you mean 'Chloe's in the hospital'?" I turn on the light. "Is she okay?" I ask, getting out of bed and going over to my suitcase, where I begin tossing all of my belongings inside.

"Shit." He takes a deep breath. "Duane was keeping an eye on her in the bar and noticed that she'd started acting strange. She went to the restroom and he followed her, so when she didn't reappear after a few minutes, he went in and found her unconscious on the floor of one of the stalls. Right now, we're waiting for the doctor to tell us what's going on."

"What the fuck happened?" I growl, powering up my computer. I need to get in touch with my pilot to ready the jet. I need to get to Chloe.

"We're not sure. I'm pulling the video from the bar as we speak."

"Stay with her until I get there. Do not let her out of your sight," I command.

"Will do, sir," he replies immediately.

"The jet will be in the air within the hour. If you hear anything, let me know right away," I tell him while texting my pilot.

"You have my word," he says.

I hang up and go to my suitcase to pull out a pair of jeans and a T-shirt, getting dressed quickly before zipping up my bag. Then I pull my phone out and head down to the lobby of the hotel. As soon as I reach the front entrance, I call Wesly and quickly let him know that I'm on my way back to the US and I will be calling Mr. Yakamora. I'll need to explain that I had to leave Japan immediately and any business we need to discuss can be taken care of via conference call.

I won't be leaving Chloe again, even if I have to handcuff her to me.

"CAN I TAKE your coat?" the flight attendant asks.

I hand it to her and pull out my phone from my pocket when it begins to ring. "Yes?"

"Sir, I wanted to give you an update. The doctor has her on an IV, and they are running a few more tests, but they believe she was drugged with Zolpide and she had an allergic reaction to it."

"Who the fuck was close enough to her to drug her?" I demand.

"Sir, I'm not sure," Ricket says quietly.

"Can I speak with her?"

"She hasn't woken up yet," he says almost under his breath, and a ball of hot rage fills my chest.

"Call me the moment she wakes up," I hiss, running a shaky hand through my hair, "and for fuck's sake, find out what the fuck happened!" I shout, clicking off the phone.

By the time we land in New York, my anxiety level has tripled. Chloe still hasn't woken up and there is no evidence on the tapes showing that anyone had the opportunity to drug her.

It takes an hour to make it from the private airstrip in Westchester to the hospital in downtown Manhattan, where Chloe is. As soon as I pull up outside of the hospital, Ricket is there to meet my town car. Without a word, I follow him into the hospital, and as soon as I step off the elevator, my hackles rise. Maxine is standing in the hall with a man I have never seen before.

"What are you doing here?" I ask her as soon as I get within speaking distance.

Her head turns towards me and she smiles. "I thought it would be best if I met you here," she says quietly and starts to reach out her hand to touch me.

I instantly pull away. "You thought wrong. You can go," I tell her, taking a step towards Chloe's room, but the man who was standing with her steps in front of me, blocking my path. "I suggest you move aside," I tell him.

"Do you now?" he asks and steps in front of me again when I try to move around him.

If I weren't exhausted from traveling and worrying, I would lay the kid out, but as it stands, he may be able to get one over on me.

"Sir, this is Chloe's boyfriend," Maxine says from beside me, and I turn to look at her then back at him.

"The only man in Chloe's life is me. Now get the fuck out of my way," I bark.

He opens his mouth and begins to speak, but one of my men steps in, wrapping his hand around the guy's arm. He starts to struggle but quickly stops when my man leans down and says something to him.

I turn towards Chloe's room then stop and look over my shoulder. "Bernard."

My bodyguard stops and turns to look at me as well as the guy. "Yes, boss?" he asks, looking back at me.

"I want to know everything about him, and make sure he understands he is not allowed to even breathe the same air as Chloe again," I tell him.

He lifts his chin and starts to lead the guy away.

"Now, you," I say, turning towards Maxine before heading into Chloe's room. "If I find out you've somehow had a hand in all this shit, you will pray I end you."

"Nolan," she whispers, and I shake my head.

"Get out, now," I snarl.

She jumps slightly before quickly turning and walking away. I take a breath and stretch my neck before stepping into the room where Chloe is.

The TV is on, blue light casting a glow around the room. My eyes go to the bed, and I take my angel in before stepping towards her. The blankets are tucked around her, her hands at her sides. Her eyes are closed, her dark lashes lying over her cheekbones. Her hair is up, and I can tell she styled it by the way the curls are still holding in her normally straight hair. I walk towards her and see that one of her hands has an IV attached. It feels like it takes forever to make it the ten steps to her side. My hand instantly goes to her face, and my fingers travel down her jaw when I see a large bruise there.

"Jesus, Angel. What the fuck happened?" I whisper, looking her over. I can't believe this happened to her. I slip off my shoes and climb into the bed with her, being careful not to move her too much as I wrap myself around her.

"Nolan," Chloe says as I feel her fingers travel though my hair.

I smile and open my eyes a crack. As the events of the last twenty-eight hours come back to me, the smile disappears and my eyes open completely, meeting Chloe's concerned ones.

"Angel." I swallow, gently pulling her closer so I can press my lips to her forehead.

"Why am I here?" she whimpers, and I can hear the tears in her voice.

I pull slightly away from her so I can look into her eyes. "You got sick and passed out in the bathroom of the club."

"I told them I didn't want to drink," she says faintly, making me instantly annoyed with the people she had gone out with. I should have known better than to trust anyone with her care.

"It's okay," I say, sitting up on the side of the bed while pressing the call button for the doctor. Then I slip on my shoes.

"Are you okay?" she asks, and the touch of her hand causes me to let out a sharp breath.

I'm so maddened by the thought of what could have happened to her that I could kill. I turn towards her and push my own personal demons aside. She needs me now, and I cannot let my own emotions overrule that.

"Fine, Beautiful," I tell her, running a hand over her hair.

"Sir," Ricket says, which is followed by someone else's, "You're awake."

When I turn my head, an attractive man a few years younger than I am walks in wearing a set of dark-blue scrubs.

"I'm Alex, Chloe's nurse." He smiles, looking at Chloe a little too long before his eyes meet mine at me.

"We're fine, Ricket. Thank you," I say, watching him leave before turning to look at Alex.

"I'm going to get the doctor. Do you need anything before that?" he asks Chloe, taking a step closer to the bed.

"I need to use the restroom," Chloe says softly, her cheeks turning slightly pink.

"I can help you with that," he says, but I block his way.

"You just get the doctor. I'll make sure she makes it to the restroom," I snarl, and a smile twitches his lips, making a growl vibrate my chest.

"Let me just unhook her IV. That way, it's a little easier for you," he says.

I want to tell him no, but I know that, logically, that doesn't make sense, so I reluctantly step aside so he can get to Chloe. It only takes a second for him to get her unhooked, and then he leaves the room.

"I can walk," she complains as I pick her up and carry her into the bathroom.

"Not yet," I tell her, helping her to the toilet. I stand at my full height over her, and her eyes narrow.

"You don't need to wait in here with me. I'm fine," she says.

I sigh, shaking my head. "Until the doctor says otherwise, you're not to be left alone."

"I hate when you get bossy," she grumbles.

I shrug. She can find it annoying all day long, but it won't change anything.

After she finishes in the bathroom and I help her wash her hands, I carry her back to bed just in time for the doctor to walk into the room followed by Nurse Alex.

"Miss Kasters," Chloe's doctor says, coming to stand next to the bed, "how are you feeling?"

Chloe looks from the doctor, to me, then back again. "A little out of it," she frowns.

The doctor nods and looks down at the tablet in her hand. "That's understandable. Your blood results came back, and it appears you had quite a bit of the drug Ambien in your system."

"Isn't that sleeping medication?" Chloe asks, and I take her hand in mine.

"Yes, but it's also used as a predator drug."

"Do you mean like a date rape drug?" Chloe asks, and her nails dig into my skin.

"Unfortunately, yes," the doctor replies softly.

"Did I…" Chloe whispers then pauses to look at me.

The fear and confusion I see in her eyes has me moving so I can hold her face between my hands. "No, Beautiful," I reply on a hoarse whisper. "You passed out in the bathroom at the club, but no one touched you."

Her eyes close, and I pull her closer to me, placing my lips to her forehead.

"No one touched you," I repeat against her skin.

She nods, and I sit back.

"I know this is very upsetting, but everything seems to be fine now." The doctor smiles softly at Chloe.

"How long must she stay here?"

"I would like to monitor her for the next two hours. If she doesn't show any signs of having a concussion, I'll release her."

She looks from me to Chloe and lowers her voice. "I need you to let me know if anything changes over the next seventy-two hours. You have been asleep for a long time, but we believe that it was due to the amount of Ambien in your system."

"Maybe it would be best if she stays here," I state, not wanting to risk something happening to her while out of the hospital.

"I'm fine," Chloe says, and I look at her then back at the doctor.

"Are you sure it's a good idea to send her home?" I ask, watching a smile twitch her lips as Chloe cuts me off with, "I'll be okay."

I let out a breath and look at my angel. I despise that this has happened, and I don't know how I'm going to function. Since I met Chloe, I have felt the need to protect her. Now, with this turn of events, I feel that urge getting stronger.

"If the doctor says you should stay, you're staying," I state, leaving no room for an argument.

"She already said I could go home," Chloe says, and I hear a chuckle from either the doctor or "Alex the Nurse" and ignore it.

"Maybe we should get a second opinion," I grumble under my breath.

"Nolan, that's ridiculous," she states, rolling her eyes.

I begin to wonder if she hasn't really hurt herself. I can't remember Chloe ever being so defiant.

"She just told you I'm okay. If anything changes, I can come back."

"Okay," I say and then look at the doctor. "I'll need the number for an at-home nurse.

"Nolan," Chloe chimes in.

"No," I assert, swinging my head in her direction. "If you're coming home, we're doing it my way."

She must understand from my tone that this is not something I will budge on, because she instantly jerks her head in an up-and-down motion.

"Now, if that's everything, she needs her rest until you release her," I bark, looking from Chloe, to her doctor, and then to Alex.

I know it makes no sense to be angry, and I'm not mad at Chloe—I'm mad at this situation. Being who I am, I'm used to having control, and this situation is completely out of my hands. I know I won't be able to rest easy until I find out who tried to hurt my angel.

"I will be back to bring you your discharge papers. If things look good when I get back, I'll sign you out."

"Thank you," Chloe says. Then she looks at me and raises an eyebrow, causing me to press my lips together. "Nolan," she whispers and elbows me in the ribs.

I look at the doctor and mutter a quick, "Thank you," before watching her and Nurse Alex leave the room.

The moment they are out of sight, Chloe looks at me.

"What?" I ask, putting her feet up on the bed.

"You were so rude," she huffs, flopping back onto the pillow.

"Careful," I bark, and her eyes go wide, causing me to flinch. "You were drugged. Your face is bruised and you have been unconscious for the last twenty-four hours, so don't look at me like you're surprised I'm reacting this way."

"I know," she sighs, and my eyes meet hers, "but I'm okay."

Her hand comes up to run along my jaw. My hand covers hers and I turn my head to kiss her palm. I know she's right, but that doesn't make it any easier. I nod and finish tucking her into bed before kissing her forehead and going out into the hall to talk to

Ricket.

"Sir," Ricket says as soon as he sees me walk out of Chloe's room.

"Where's Bernard?"

"He—"

"I'm here," Bernard announces, walking around the corner.

"Any news?"

"Not yet." He shakes his head, looking towards Chloe's room. "How's she doing?"

"Better," I tell him, running a hand down the back of my neck.

"So, no news on who the guy was either?"

"When I spoke to him outside, he said he was Chloe's boyfriend from high school."

"Why the fuck is he showing up here now?"

"Said he got a call from someone saying she was in the hospital. He told me he and Chloe have kept in contact over the years and he has always thought of her as his girl, so he wanted to make sure she was okay."

The words "his girl" ring in my ears and I try to steady my breathing as my hands clench into fists.

"I want you to find out everything on him down to what he ate for breakfast this morning, and I don't want him anywhere near Chloe. I don't even want him to catch a glimpse of her."

"My men will be keeping a close eye on him."

"Make sure," I growl before turning on my heel and heading back to Chloe. I know it's not my men's fault that this happened, but fear of the unknown has me lashing out. I just need some answers sooner rather than later.

CHAPTER 3

"WHAT ARE YOU doing?" I bark, walking into the bathroom, where Chloe is submerged in the tub with her eyes closed and mounds of white bubbles surrounding her.

"Taking a bath," she answers, not even opening her eyes.

"You could drown," I tell her, walking to her and picking her up out of the water, not caring when my clothes become soaked by doing so.

"Put me down, Nolan."

"No. You're going to bed," I say, ignoring her struggles as I grab a towel with one hand before leaving the bathroom and carrying her to the bed, where she was supposed to be while I went to make a few phone calls.

"You are being ridiculous. First, you carry me around like a doll, and now, I can't take a bath?" she cries, glaring at me.

"It was safer for me to carry you." I shrug and start to dry her off, but she pulls the towel from my hand and starts whipping it at me, causing me to dodge her while trying to take it from her without hurting her in the process. "Chloe, stop. You'll hurt yourself," I say, finally getting the towel from her hands.

She reaches down to the end of the bed and grabs the blanket, pulling it over herself before crossing her arms over her chest and letting out a long huff.

"You're supposed to be resting."

"I was resting." She rolls her eyes, suddenly getting out of bed.

"Now, what are you doing?"

"I need something to sleep in," she mutters, walking past me to the dresser, opening my top drawer, and grabbing a shirt out.

"Are you hungry?" I ask, watching her slip my T-shirt over her head. I stand there hard as a rock as the shirt slides over her perfect tits, past the soft roundness of her stomach, and then down to cover her bare pussy.

"I'm still not hungry," she says when her head turns and our eyes meet.

I watch as longing flashes in her eyes, and she starts towards me slowly.

"Angel," I warn, and her step falters slightly before she continues her path. This time, the sway of her hips has my cock begging to reach her.

"I missed you." Her voice drops and her hand goes to my chest, causing my already hard cock to become almost unbearable.

"You need your rest."

"I need you," she hisses, her hand at my chest traveling down my stomach, cupping me, her small fingers trying to wrap around my cock through the material of my pants.

"No." I take her hand and wrap my arm around her waist, gently pulling her closer to me. "You're not well."

"I'm fine," she moans, and by the noise she's making and the slight movement of her thighs, I know she's running hot.

"I decide when you're well enough to fuck," I whisper near her ear, and she whimpers as my hand slides around then down her stomach. "Do you want to come?" I know I can't fuck her like I crave to, but I never want her to want for anything, even if it's just an orgasm.

Her cheek moves against my chest, and she mewls as my fingers slide between the lips of her pussy.

"Poor Angel," I say, feeling how swollen she is as my fingers begin to slowly circle her clit then move down over her entrance.

Her hips begin to move with my hand, and she's so wet that my fingers are sliding with no resistance.

"Did you miss me?" I groan, sliding two fingers deep inside her, pressing against her G-spot. I can feel pre-cum coating the tip of my cock and know I'm making a fucking mess of myself. "Answer me," I snarl when she doesn't answer.

"Yes," she cries as I begin to fuck her fast with my fingers.

I can feel her pussy getting tighter and hotter, and I know she is going to come, but I need her taste. I walk her backwards to the bed, making sure to keep my grip around her waist, my fingers never losing their rhythm. Once I have her to the bed, I gently lean her back onto the mattress, covering her body with mine.

I lift my head and look down at her as her eyes open and she looks up at me. There is so much hunger, so much desire in her eyes that I lower my mouth over hers just so I can break eye contact. I know what I want to do right now, but I force myself to take control of the urge to be deep inside her. Once I get my fill of her mouth, I gently move down her neck, using my free hand to lift my shirt she's wearing and expose her breasts.

The cool air hits her nipples, causing them to tighten even more. The fingers I'm using to stroke inside her lift up, causing her back to arch off the bed, raising her breasts closer to my mouth. I blow a warm puff of air over her nipple before laving it with my tongue and blowing another breath across it. Then I pull it deep into my mouth.

Her whimper and her nails digging into my hair egg me on. Once I have given both breasts the same treatment, I kiss down her stomach, licking around her belly button before lowering myself and lifting one of her legs up and over my shoulder, spreading her out in front of me. I sit back, watching my fingers enter her in smooth strokes, then start fucking her harder with them before lowering my face to lick right up her center. I pull her sweet, pure taste into my mouth and circle her clit with my tongue before sucking it into my mouth and flicking it.

The heel of her foot digs into my shoulder, her pussy clamps down on my fingers, and her screams fill the room right before her body goes completely limp and silence fills the air. After I feel her body fully relax and know that her orgasm has passed, I slowly pull my fingers out then place them into my mouth, savoring her taste as I kiss my way back up her body. Once I reach her face, I kiss her once, seeing that her eyes are closed. They slowly flutter open, and a small smile forms on her mouth.

"Sleep, Angel," I tell her as I fix her shirt and adjust her in the bed.

I cover her up before pulling off my own shirt while heading to the bathroom, where I'm extra careful about removing my pants. I'm still so hard that it's almost painful. I make quick work in the shower and dry off hastily. I don't even bother with clothes before crawling into bed with Chloe and pulling her against my chest. Then I fall asleep.

"I SHOULD GO to work," Chloe says.

I lift my head from the papers I've been going over for a case so I can glare at her. She has been repeating the same thing for the last three days. I do not know how many times I need to tell her that it's not happening before she'll get it. Hell, she will be lucky to go back to work at all.

"We've spoken about this."

"*You've* spoken about this." She rolls her eyes before standing from the table and heading for the kitchen. "I need to work. I need to make money so I can pay my bills," she says, and anger instantly ignites in my stomach.

"I have plenty of money."

"I know, but that's your money."

"I will take care of you."

"Nolan, I love you, but I was never looking for a sugar daddy," she cries, throwing her hands up in the air.

"Chloe, watch it," I snarl. "You're really testing my patience," I say, tossing the papers in my hands down onto the table before standing from the chair, hearing it hit the wall behind me.

"Nolan." She swallows.

"I'm the one who got a phone call from halfway across the world telling me the woman I love had been drugged. I'm the one that happened to, so you do *not* get to make this seem like I'm trying to keep you here for my own satisfaction. I'm keeping you here because it's safe," I rumble, leaning my head back in frustration.

She has become more and more defiant, and the way I would normally get her to submit cannot occur at this time—not until I know she is completely okay.

"I'm sorry," she whispers. My head lowers and our eyes meet.

"I just need to get out of the house. I mean, you didn't even tell me you were moving me in with you. Yesterday, all my stuff just showed up here."

Okay, so I may have gone a little bit overboard, but given the circumstances, I was tired of waiting, and now, I fully believe that the only place she is safe is with me. So that is where she will be from now on. And no, I do not want to be her sugar daddy, but the job has to go. If I need to travel for business, she is going to come with me. I will no longer be able to leave her while I'm out of town.

"I need to know you're safe."

"Before meeting you, nothing like this has ever happened to me," she whispers as her head lowers and her hands wring together.

Her words feel like a steel pipe going right through my gut. I hate the idea of being the one who has caused her to be harmed. I've only ever wanted to take care of her.

"Come here, Beautiful," I sigh while opening my arms, and she walks to me, shoving her face into my chest as her arms wrap around me tightly. "I should have spoken to you about moving your stuff in, but I knew you would try to tell me, again, that it's too soon. I removed the choice from your hands and did what needed to be done."

Her head tilts back, and I gather some of her hair at the back of her head into my hand, making a fist. I then lower my mouth to hers, slipping my tongue between her lips, calling hers to come out and play. When she moans and her body rises higher, I pull away, placing one more gentle kiss on her lips before pulling her head back into my chest.

"What would you like to do today?" I ask after a moment of

standing in silence.

Her head tilts back again and her face lights up. "I've never been to the Museum of Natural History."

Internally, I groan, knowing that the place is likely overrun with children right now. But if my angel wants to go to the museum, then I suppose that is what we're going to do.

"All right. Go get ready while I finish up some work. We'll leave in an hour."

"Really?" She smiles bigger, and my mouth lowers again, kissing that one off her lips.

"Really," I reply against her mouth before pulling away and turning her towards the stairs, where I watch until she disappears out of sight.

"There are a lot of kids here," Chloe says as we make our way through the dinosaur exhibits.

"Most of the schools in the five boroughs bring the kids to this museum during the week, and then you have all the nannies who bring the kids here during the day. Or moms who just want something to do with their rug rats show up here as well," I tell her, wrapping my arm around her shoulders so I can lead us though the crowd.

"I had no idea," she mutters.

"When I was growing up, I only liked coming here for one reason." I lead her past some of the exhibits, heading towards my favorite spot in the building.

"Holy cow," she breathes, looking up at the giant blue whale that takes up a huge expanse of the museum.

"I used to lie on the ground under it for hours," I tell her, looking around.

The area the whale is kept is dark and the floor is empty, making it the perfect spot to get away from all the noise inside the museum. I lead her towards the middle of the floor and watch as she looks around the room. There are kids everywhere along with adults who are looking at the displays tucked into the walls.

"Come on." She pulls my hand, beginning to sit on the floor.

I frown down at her. "What are you doing?"

"Come on, old man. I need the full experience." She laughs, sitting down completely before lying on the floor.

I shake my head but follow her down, resting my head near hers. She moves my arm and lays her head on my chest.

"This is so cool," she whispers.

I squeeze her shoulder. I forgot how much I enjoyed doing this when I was young.

"This is where I had my first kiss," I say, kissing her forehead.

"Was she your girlfriend?" Her cheek moves against my chest, and I know she's smiling.

"I was six. I thought she was my girlfriend, so when we came for a field trip, I kissed her when we got to this part of the museum."

"What did she do?" She giggles, making me smile.

"She hit me then ran off and told the teacher."

"Your poor ego." She tilts her head back, and the soft look in her eyes makes me realize that this is the spot I will ask her to marry me once the ring I'm having made for her is complete.

"I survived," I mutter, pulling her face up towards mine.

She instantly rises up on her elbow and lowers her mouth down to mine, nibbling my bottom lip before licking it. My hand moves to hold her face to take over the kiss, but we're suddenly interrupted.

"Dere kissin'!" a kid yells, and a bunch of giggles break out around us.

Both Chloe's face and mine turn at the same time to see that there is a group of kids who are all wearing matching shirts and look to be around five standing around us and laughing.

"Oh my God," Chloe whispers and hides her face in my chest.

I lay my head back down, break out into laughter, and can feel Chloe shaking from doing the same.

"I think we need to get up," I tell her, sitting up and seeing that the children have moved on.

We spend the next few hours walking around the museum, checking out different displays before heading out of the building. Once on the street, I signal to Ricket as we walk towards the park.

"This is nice," Chloe mutters.

I look down at her as she takes a bite of the pretzel I just bought her. I forget sometimes to step back from work to just enjoy the little moments.

"It has been nice," I agree, bending my head to take a bite of her pretzel, making her laugh.

By the time we arrive back at my penthouse, it is dark. There is a chill in the air, and Chloe is shivering. She insisted we walk instead of taking the car, so I sent Ricket ahead of us, telling him that he could have the night off. That's why I'm surprised to find him waiting in the lobby of the building along with Bernard.

"Sir," Ricket says when he spots me.

"Is everything okay?" I ask, rubbing Chloe's arm, trying to warm her up. We both dressed light to go out, and now, I wish I would have brought a jacket or demanded we take the car home.

"Evening," Bernard says to Chloe before moving his eyes to mine. "We need to meet."

I nod. "Let me get Chloe upstairs and warmed up, and then we can talk," I tell him, watching as he lifts his chin and follows us to the elevator.

Once I have Chloe in the bath, I make my way out to the living room, where Bernard and Ricket are both speaking quietly.

"Tell me what's going on," I say, pouring a glass of scotch.

"I have gone over the videos from the club again from the night Chloe was drugged and still have not found even one moment when she could have been slipped the drug. Throughout the evening, she was never away from the other women at the event, she never went to the bar alone, and the party she was with had pitchers of drinks brought to them, and none of the other women ever showed any signs of having been given the same thing as Chloe."

"The drug was in her system, and I know she has never taken sleeping medication, so at some point during that party, she was given the drug," I growl.

"I agree," Bernard says then looks at Ricket. "What I'm thinking is one of the women at the party slipped it into her drink. They are the only ones who would have had the opportunity to do so. My men were watching her the entire evening, and at no point was anyone who wasn't part of the bachelorette party even within sneezing distance of her."

"So you believe one of the women she was with drugged her?" I shake my head. "That makes no sense at all."

"I don't know why someone did it, but women from the party are the only ones who would have had the opportunity to do so."

"So, what's the plan?" I look in the direction of the bathroom, not wanting Chloe to come out during this talk. I don't want her to even know there is something going on or what they suspect. I don't know how she would react if she knew they believe that her friends had something to do with her being drugged.

"Right now, I'm gathering all the information I can on the women who attended the party. So far, they are all coming up as a bunch of well-to-do trophy wives, and I cannot find any link that would lead me to believe they would hold a grudge against her."

"Chloe is innocent. I believe whatever's going on here has more to do with me than her."

"You think someone is using her to get to you?" Bernard replies, and I nod. "That would make sense. I have been going the ex-boyfriend route, but even he has been a dead end."

"What do you mean?"

"He went home. He hasn't even tried to contact her."

"So why did he show up here?"

"I have my guy looking into his phone records. I want to find out how he knew Chloe was in the hospital. Someone had to have contacted him to give him that information."

"For what purpose?"

"Sir, if I may," Ricket speaks, and I turn to look at my old friend. "You're very possessive of Ms. Kasters. Perhaps whomever did this believed you would do something rash."

"Like what?"

"Perhaps leave, sir," Ricket says.

Memories of my marriage come back to me. I never even asked my ex if she was having an affair—not that I needed to. But even if all of the evidence hadn't been right there in front of me, I still wouldn't have given her a chance to explain.

I have never been the most understanding person. Chloe hasn't been in my life for long, so if someone were trying to make me believe she was playing me, was having a relationship with someone else, and didn't understand the depth of emotions I feel for her, they may have thought they could make me believe them.

What they don't know is I'm obsessed with her, and there is nothing anyone can do, including her, that would deter me from keeping her.

"How long will it take to get the phone records?"

"It will take a few days. Phone records are a little more difficult."

"Let me know what you find out as soon as you have the information."

"You know I will," Bernard answers, patting my arm before heading towards the front door.

"Would you like me to do anything, sir?" Ricket inquires.

"No. Just have a good night. Tomorrow, I will need to go into the office for a few hours. I'll call when I'm ready to leave," I tell him, and he nods once before heading towards the front door.

Once I know they are gone, I head towards the bedroom to check on Chloe. There is a lot to think about, but I know that my men will be able to handle it.

CHAPTER 4

"**N**OLAN!" CHLOE YELLS, and I lean my head back to look at the ceiling before letting out a long breath.

She has been on a rampage since coming home a few hours ago, and I'm ready to spank her ass. This morning, I told her not to go to work, and I believed she agreed with me and was going to stay home. But it seems my beautiful girl has become hard of hearing, because an hour after I arrived at my office, I received a phone call from Bernard informing me that Chloe had been spotted leaving the building by one of his men, who had then proceeded to follow her, making sure she arrived at the bakery safely before posting up outside until I could meet him there.

As soon as I received this information, I ended my meeting early and met Ricket downstairs so I could pick Chloe up myself. Even if she didn't care about her safety, I did, and there was no fucking way I was taking a chance with her being at a location that is completely open where, at any time, anyone could get to her.

After I arrived at the bakery, Chloe ran into the back kitchen. At that point, I should have known she wasn't going to make it easy. It took ten minutes to corner her. I have to say that, even if she is tiny, she is fast. It didn't end with me catching her; no, I ended up carrying her kicking and screaming out of the bakery and into the back of my car. I was surprised the police didn't show up after the scene she'd caused. If it hadn't been for her injuries, I would have spanked her ass for the stunt she'd pulled.

"Nolan!" she yells again.

This time, I hear her stomping down the hall. I sit back against the couch and wait to see what happens.

"I know you can hear me," she huffs, coming to stand in front of me.

"It's hard not to hear you when you're yelling, Angel," I mutter flatly, closing up my computer.

"Don't 'Angel' me," she growls, throwing her hands up in the air. "Where are my clothes?"

"In the closet," I say slowly, wondering if she's really lost it.

"No, they're not," she huffs, blowing a piece of hair out of her face.

"Angel."

"Don't freakin' 'Angel' me! What? Did you take them so I wouldn't have anything to wear or have a way to leave the house again unless I was willing to go naked?"

"Though that does sound like a win-win, no."

"Well then, someone has stolen my clothes." She throws up her hands again before lowering them to her hips.

"Chloe, you must really want a spanking. You have been doing things all day to provoke me." I rub between my eyes and look up at her only after she has been quiet for far too long.

"I'm not lying. All of my clothes, everything of mine, is gone," she whispers.

Seeing the panicked look on her face has me standing and heading to the bedroom and into the closet. As soon as I hit the bedroom, a familiar smell hits my nose, but it's gone before I can place it. I storm to the closet and see that all of her hangers are empty. I open and close drawers, coming up with nothing. Everything is gone. My angel has a lot of clothes, and there is nothing left—not even a stray pair of panties.

I leave her standing in the closet and go to the bathroom where she keeps all her girly shit. It's all gone as well. I search our home from top to bottom, but everything of hers is gone. There is not even a sign of her left. If she weren't standing right in front of me, I would think she had disappeared. When I turn around, Chloe is standing in the middle of the kitchen with her hands covering her mouth. That's when I realize what I must look like. I can tell that my face is red-hot with anger and my body has expanded. I have no idea who the fuck came into our home, but when I find out, they are going to fucking pay.

"Come here," I demand.

She walks across the marble floors. As soon as she is within reach, I pick her up and carry her with me into the living room, where I sit down with her in my lap before pulling out my phone and calling Bernard.

"Shhhh, Angel," I whisper to the top of her head and pull her firmly against me when I hear her sob.

"Boss?" Bernard answers.

"Get your ass up to my place now," I order then hang up. "We'll get you all new clothes," I tell her, and she shakes her head, causing her face to slide against my shirt.

"Why would someone take my stuff?"

"Let's not talk about that right now," I say softly, kissing the top of her head.

My mind is traveling rapidly, and I don't want to explore the reason why until Bernard gets here. All I can think about is the fact that she left this morning, and that is when the people must have come in to take all of her stuff. I wonder what they would have done if she had been here alone. There is no telling what would have happened then. My building is secure, but just like any location, there is always room for improvement.

It takes three minutes for the phone to ring and them to tell me that they are sending a guest up. Chloe jumps at the noise and I shush her again before sitting her on the couch next to me so I can meet Bernard at the entryway.

"I'll be right around the corner. Sit here until I come back," I tell her, kissing her forehead. "Look at me, Beautiful." I place two fingers under her chin, raising her eyes to mine. "It will all be okay."

"I know," she whispers and then looks over my shoulder when the bell goes off again.

"I'll be right back."

She nods, and I kiss her lips before heading towards the door.

"What's going on?" Bernard asks as soon as I open the front door.

I lead him back down the hall towards the living room, not wanting Chloe to be out of sight for more than a moment.

"All of Chloe's belongings are gone," I tell him over my shoulder.

"How is that possible?"

"I would like to know the same thing." I run a hand through my hair and walk to the living room, finding Chloe where I left her, but now, her eyes are on her phone in her hand, her face white as a ghost.

"What's wrong?"

"I just got an e-mail," she whispers and then lifts her eyes to meet mine. "What happened when you were in Japan?" Her bottom lip trembles and tears fill her eyes.

My stomach twists as I wonder what she could possibly be talking about. "What's in the e-mail?" I coax.

She lifts her phone up towards me. The image on the screen is of me from the night I flew home when I found out she was in the hospital. I'm sitting in one of the chairs, and the angle the picture was taken makes it appear like the waitress and I are kissing.

I remember that moment. I had been taking a drink from the waitress, and she had bent down towards me to ask a question, so I had leaned forward to hear her more clearly.

"That isn't what it looks like," I state, taking a step towards her. "Do not ever question the depth of emotions I feel for you. I would never disrespect you or us like that."

Her eyes search my face, and she swallows before lowering her face towards her phone again. For a moment, I wonder if whoever is doing this has won, if they have succeeded in taking away the most important thing in my life. Then her phone clicks off, her eyes meet mine, and I see that she's still with me, and the knot in my stomach unravels.

"I will find out who's doing this and bury them," I vow, turning towards Bernard. "I want to know who was here and how the fuck they got in. In the meantime, I'm taking Chloe to my house upstate. I want three men with us. I expect that, by the time I talk to you next, you have some kind of lead," I tell him before turning back to Chloe and holding out my hand for her.

She takes it and I pull her up off the couch.

"Is Ricket driving you?" Bernard asks.

My first instinct is to say yes, but I think driving may help ease what I'm currently feeling. "I'm driving," I reply, picking up my briefcase and car keys from the table beside the door.

As soon as we're inside, I press the button for the garage then pull Chloe closer, rubbing her back. Her body melts into mine and I press a kiss to the top of her head while taking a deep breath of her scent. As soon as the elevator doors open, I turn left and head straight to my favorite car: my Aston Martin Vanquish.

"I had no idea you even owned a car," Chloe says quietly while putting on her safety belt.

"Seven," I inform her, starting up the engine, the loud roar bouncing off the concrete walls.

"Seven?" She looks at me questionably.

"Seven cars, Beautiful."

"You never drive," she states, looking at me like I'm crazy.

"In the city, no, but when I go to my house upstate, I drive."

"I didn't even know you owned a house upstate," she mumbles.

"There was no reason to bring it up. I haven't been to my old house in months. I have always stayed in the city. But my parents live near there and insisted I buy it when the market bottomed out. They wanted somewhere for me to raise a family that was close to them. I'm sure we would have gone sometime soon. My mother can only be put off for so long. You know she has been chomping at the bit to meet you since you answered my phone when you saw her name appear on the caller ID." I smile at the memory.

"Who keeps their parents saved in their phone under their real names?" she mutters, and despite the situation, I can't help but laugh.

"She got a good laugh out of it." I squeeze her hand.

"In all fairness, there were a lot of girls calling before that." She sighs.

"Then you came along and I couldn't see past you. I still can't see past you."

"I love you." She places her hand on mine. The words "I love you" always feel so inadequate for what I feel for her.

"Love you too, Beautiful." I bring her hand to my mouth and press a kiss there. "I don't want you worrying. I want you to trust me to take care of you and to keep you safe."

"I just wish I knew why all of this is happening."

"You were right earlier. This has nothing to do with you. This is all because of me."

"What did you do?"

"I'm not sure, Angel, but in life, sometimes all you have to do is be breathing in order to piss people off."

"That makes no sense," she replies softly, leaning her head over onto my shoulder.

The rest of the drive is silent, with Chloe asleep while I go over potential suspects in my head. I know I have made enemies doing the work I do, but none of them would ever be so personal in their revenge. Women of my past flash through my head, but I can't see any of them doing this.

My mind keeps venturing towards Maxine, the way she has acted and the things she's said to me regarding Chloe, but I believe my relationship with her father would deter her from doing anything like this. I have no main suspect, no real reason for this turn of events. Nothing like this ever occurred when I dated in the past.

We pull up to my house after an hour, and Chloe sleepily lifts her head when I move her to punch in the code for the gate.

"This isn't a house," she says.

I turn my head to look at the structure in front of us. It's all brick, with three-story, white pillars that line the front porch. It's ten thousand square feet, eight bedrooms, nine baths, with a rec room and two large living rooms.

"I know it's big, but I plan to fill every room in that house with a kid someday."

"And who exactly is going to have that many kids?"

"You." I smile when I see her shake her head out of the corner of my eye while I pull into the garage.

"Do I get a say in it?" Chloe asks, raising an eyebrow.

"You had a say the first night I walked you home. That was the time for you to run, but instead, you took my hand and let me get a taste of you. Now, I'm fucking addicted, and now, not even you can stop me from getting what I want," I declare.

She surprises me by leaning over and pressing a kiss to my lips before quickly getting out of the car. I turn off the engine and shut the door for the garage while I'm still in the car, and then I unhook my belt before opening the door and getting out. Chloe is standing at the rear of the car as I pull off my suit jacket, laying it over the trunk then pulling my belt loose. I hold it in one hand while the other one grabs Chloe around the waist, jerking her towards me.

"My beautiful angel," I mutter, crashing my mouth down onto hers while pulling her hands behind her back.

Her moan is the exact sound I want to hear as I use my belt to quickly bind her hands. Once she's bound, I lift her, placing her on my jacket.

"Nolan," she gasps as I slip her shoes off. Then I rip open her jeans, pull them over her hips, and toss them to the ground behind me.

"No talking," I snarl as I lift her legs from behind her knees and pull her ass towards the edge. "Do you see, Chloe?" I growl, using my fingers under her chin to pull her face towards me. "Do you understand that, when you continue to give yourself to me willingly, you constantly feed the addiction I have for you?" I travel my hands up her thighs, to her waist, then up under her shirt, pulling it over her head in the process. "But, for you, there is no cure, no treatment," I rumble against her mouth, licking it before licking down her neck to the tops of her breasts, pulling down the cups of her bra, and then stepping back to look at her.

"Open," I say, placing my thumb in her mouth, swirling it around her tongue. Once it's coated nicely, I pull it free, immediately placing it on her clit, using her saliva and juices for lubrication smoothly to circle it. "Put your feet on the trunk and stay open for me," I order, never stopping my ministrations.

Once she's positioned like I want, I kiss her in approval, showing her what I will soon be doing with my mouth to her pussy. She cries out as I twist her nipple while thrusting deep into her soaking-wet sex. I slowly pull away from the kiss so I can watch her face as she comes.

Her pussy tightens around my fingers as her eyes roll back into her head. Before her orgasm even passes, I lower my face, keeping my rhythm deep inside her while swallowing all of her juices. When her body begins to tremble, I know she is going to go over again, so I make a quick decision, using one hand to pull myself free.

My cock is rock hard, throbbing with anticipation, knowing

that, soon, it will be surrounded by hot, wet silk. There is nothing better than being inside her, nothing better than knowing that her pussy was made to take only my cock. Since taking her virginity, I swear my cock was designed to fit inside her like the perfect puzzle piece.

I thrust slowly at first, then faster, watching my length disappear. Her tits are bouncing over the top of her bra with each thrust. Her knees start to shake as her pussy begins to ripple around my girth, and when I know she's on the verge of coming, I pull out and bury my face between her legs so she can orgasm on my tongue. Then I stand, sliding back inside her hard and fast, making the car rock.

Her cry of ecstasy eggs me on, making me fuck into her wildly until my balls draw up and I force her face to mine.

"One more. Give me one more," I growl, forcing my tongue down her throat as long jets of come shoot off inside her, filling her womb with my seed, setting off her third orgasm.

Her body goes limp, and I pull her to my chest, running my hand down her back then releasing the belt from her wrists. It takes a few minutes for her to come back to me, but the first thing she does is kiss my chest, cuddling closer to me. This is why my addiction for her grows. She accepts me, all of me, while asking for even more.

I tilt her head back and place a soft kiss on her lips before slipping out of her and fixing my pants. Then I look at her clothes, which are now in a pile on the floor, and take off my shirt, putting it on her before lifting her under her ass and wrapping her legs around my waist.

"Okay, Angel. Let's show you your new home," I say, carrying her to the door.

I should have brought her here a long time ago. When I knew what she meant to me, I should have kidnapped her ass and brought her here, where I could have kept her to myself and we could have started our lives without ever giving anyone the opportunity to fuck with us.

I carry her inside, entering right into the kitchen, where I set her down on the counter.

"Let me get you some water, and then I'm going to call my mom and have her pick you up some stuff to wear. When I know things have calmed down a little, we can go to the mall," I say, going to the fridge, pulling out a bottle of water, then bringing it to her.

"I can go," she says.

My hand with the water bottle puts it to the side then lifts her face to me. "You will not leave unless I'm with you."

"I never said I was going alone," she replies calmly, placing her hand on my cheek. "I just feel weird having your mom get me clothes."

I force my body to relax before speaking. "Don't. It will make her feel like she's helping. Would you like to take a bath?"

She nods and I pick her up again, carrying her upstairs to our bedroom. Once I have the bath full, I help her out of my shirt then watch as she lowers herself into the water.

"I think I'm going to wait a few days to call my mother," I tell her, pulling my pants off.

"Why?" she asks confused.

"If I don't call her, you have nothing to wear. I can think of worse ways to spend my days."

She bites her bottom lip then breaks out into laughter, tossing a handful of bubbles at me.

"You'll pay for that." I lunge for her, making her laugh louder.

That's the instant I realize how much I have missed that sound and vow to find a way to make her laugh every day from this day forward.

CHAPTER 5

"YOU'RE NOT WEARING that. Go and change," I growl, watching my beautiful angel walk towards me in a white dress that looks like it was designed to piss me off.

The front is hooked around her neck with some kind of choker made of crystals and gold. The fabric of the dress is attached there, just at the front of her neck, before flowing down over her breasts. Then the waist of the dress is bunched together with a belt that matches the choker. Her sides are completely exposed, showing off a large expanse of her skin, as the skirt flows to the floor. I'm sure if she turned even slightly, I would see the side of her breast. Being at a party attended by the men from my firm with her in that dress will definitely lead to me shoving my fist into someone's face when they look at her too long.

I watch as her step falters and her smile disappears.

"You sent this dress for me to wear," she mutters, looking down.

I cannot stand that she is going to be out in public in that scrap of fabric, but I *really* can't stand the look on her face right now. This is entirely my mother's fault. She has fallen in love with Chloe and loves dressing her. She was in my office when the invite showed up for the party and insisted she be the one to pick Chloe's dress. I should have known better.

"You look stunning." I step towards her, running my index finger down her bare side. "I don't know how I'm going to make it through the evening without killing every man who looks at you." *That's not a lie,* I think, tracing the edge of her breast.

"You didn't pick this, did you?" she asks.

I lift my eyes to meet hers and shake my head.

"I can change."

"No. You look…" I shake my head, trying to think of a way to describe her. "You look absolutely beautiful."

Her hair is down, framing her face. Her makeup is light, just adding to her already elegant features. And the dress, though risqué, still looks charming on her. "I'm sure to be the envy of every man there."

Her eyes narrow and she chews on her bottom lip. "Are you sure you're going to be okay?"

It's on the tip of my tongue to say no, but there is no way I can do that to her—not right now. We've been staying in Westchester for two weeks now, and since coming here, I have seen my girl come out of her shell more and more. The first week was difficult. I knew she was very worried about everything that had transpired since leaving the city, but with my family and me around, she has blossomed. I was working from home most days and spending the nights trying to implant my child inside her. Even with everything hanging over us, I feel content, more at ease than I have in a long time.

"I know it's not something I would pick for myself," Chloe says, bringing me back to the moment, "but I kind of like it." She smiles, and I know I will end up regretting this, but seeing that smile makes it somewhat worth it.

"Nolan."

I hear my name and turn my head to the left, seeing Carter standing with a tall blonde I'm sure he met sometime within the last twenty-four hours.

"Carter." I stop with my hand around Chloe's waist, trying to block her from his view.

Carter's father owns the second-largest international law firm in New York City. He went to Yale and has made a name for himself in the world of law since passing his bar exam by settling billion-dollar cases. He has also made a name for himself in the beds of women all over the city. At thirty years old, good-looking, with enough money to put Bill Gates to shame, he has women killing themselves just for a moment of his time. All of them want to be the one to turn the player into the perfect husband.

"Nolan, nice to see you." He sticks out his hand.

The blonde at his side latches on to him, her red nails digging into his suit jacket as she gives me a smile.

"Who do you have here?" he asks, his eyes zeroing in on Chloe, whose own fingers begin digging into my skin through the fabric of my suit.

"Chloe," she replies, and I look down at her, seeing that her eyes are glued to Carter's date. "His girlfriend," she adds in a tone I have never heard from my angel before.

I bite back my smile as she looks up at me and glares.

"Nice to meet you, Chloe," Carter says and begins to pull Chloe's hand to his mouth. Lucky for him, she pulls away from his grasp, helping to save his life.

"Nice to meet you, too." She smiles then looks at me. "I

would like a drink."

"Sure, Angel." I run my fingers down her bare side.

She narrows her eyes, making me smirk at her before I look back at Carter, who is looking between us curiously.

"We'll talk soon," I tell him before leading Chloe away towards the bar.

"Who is that woman?" Chloe hisses at me once we are away from the crowd.

My eyebrows pull together as I ask, "What woman?"

"The blonde."

I look around the room and see that Carter's date is watching us, and when our eyes meet, she smiles at me and her eyes heat.

"Yes, her," Chloe growls.

I gaze down at her, finding her flipping off the blonde. I grab her hand and pull it behind her back before anyone can see.

"I don't know her," I growl back. "Now, behave yourself."

"Behave?" she repeats.

"Yes. Unless you would like me to bend you over and spank you in front of all of these people for acting like a brat, I suggest you behave."

"You wouldn't." She struggles against my hold.

My arms wrap around her, turning so that my body is blocking her from the rest of the room as I slap her ass hard enough to get her attention. Her body stills and her mouth opens on a gasp.

"Now, behave," I tell her again.

"You just spanked me."

"You've been spanked by me before, Chloe. You know what a real spanking is. That was just me getting your attention."

"She keeps staring at you," she whispers, trying to look around me.

I pull her face towards me so that I have her full attention. "Where is all of this coming from?" I question, holding her cheek.

"I just don't fit in here."

"You fit in wherever I am. You outshine every person in this room. Do not ever doubt your worth," I tell her, kissing her softly. "Now, let's go get this over with so I can take you home and tie you to the bed with that dress." I smile against her mouth as she rolls her eyes.

We spend the rest of the evening mingling. Chloe has every person I introduce her to eating out of the palm of her hand with her kindness and finesse—not that I'm surprised. The qualities that draw people in are the same qualities that made me fall in love with her in the first place.

I do notice, though, that Maxine is nowhere to be seen. I transferred her the week prior to work with another lawyer after she had made a statement about Chloe to her father, telling him that, since Chloe had come into my life, she had noticed a reduction in my work and she worried that my relationship was going to affect the firm. I could no longer let her distaste for Chloe slide.

THE RIPPING SOUND of the white fabric that was covering Chloe fills the room as I tear her dress down the middle. Her eyes widen and her lips part as I lead her to the bed, positioning her in the middle with her legs spread before tying her ankles to the posts.

"This dress has driven me crazy all night," I say, running a piece of the fabric through my hands. "Watching men looking at you, watching how their eyes would heat as you spoke to them," I say, running the fabric over the tops of her breasts. "Did you enjoy that? Did you enjoy making me jealous?"

She shakes her head, and I tilt mine to look at her, searching her expression as I take one of her hands and kiss her wrist before wrapping a piece of the fabric around it.

"I believe you enjoyed it," I say, grazing a finger down her arm, over the tips of her breasts, over her belly, and then down to cup her pussy. My middle finger presses into her wetness.

"Nolan," she hisses, lifting her hips.

I press in harder, gathering some of her juices, then bring my fingers to her lips, coating them before leaning over and licking her mouth.

"So sweet," I groan into her then stand and walk around the bed to lift her other wrist to my mouth, this time sucking it before wrapping the fabric around it and tying it to the headboard. "Now, where do I start?" I smile, taking off my cufflinks, loosening my tie, and unbuttoning my shirt before shrugging it off my shoulders.

Her eyes are locked on my zipper, where my cock is outlined. I take off my belt then slowly pull down my zipper, watching her eyes. Once I'm free, I wrap my fingers around my cock and begin pumping.

"Do you want a taste?" I ask.

She nods, so I crawl up onto the bed, kneel over her face, and feed my length into her mouth and down her throat. I have taught her how to control her gag reflex, so she is a pro at taking me just the way I like.

I fuck into her mouth then use one hand to slide down her stomach and over her clit, making her hips buck. She is so wet that my fingers slip inside her with ease.

"Fuck, baby, I've got to have a taste of you," I say, causing her to moan around my cock.

Then I bury my face between her legs. My arms go around her

thighs and spread her open farther so my tongue can go deeper. I lick and suck her clit, making sure to tease her with the tips of my fingers at her entrance until she is writhing under me.

Her moans around my length make it hard to hold off my orgasm, so I move quickly, pulling out of her mouth, not wanting to waste my come down her throat. Once I'm in position, I thrust into her hard, her hands straining against the rope, and her legs shift as she fights to get loose.

"There is no place I would rather be than inside of you. Nowhere," I groan against her ear, feeling her pussy trying to suck me deeper. "Come with me, Angel. Tighten that pussy and come with me," I snarl down her throat.

Her pussy begins to milk my orgasm right from me. Then I plant myself deep and come, filling her with my seed.

"That time, I gave you my kid," I whisper, and her pussy tightens again. "You like that idea, Angel?" I ask as I lean back to look at her. I place my hands on her face to hold her gently. "Do you like the idea of having my baby?"

"Yes." She smiles as tears begin to fall into her hair.

I smile and lower my mouth to hers, kissing her once more.

Now, I just need to marry her and make it official.

"I'M SURPRISED YOU wanted to come back here," she says, laughing as we pass a group of kids on the way into the museum.

I look down at her then follow her eyes to where a little boy is licking the glass of one of the displays and shake my head. "The last time we were here made me realize how many little things I miss out on, and I don't want you to not experience things just because I'm busy.

"I don't feel like that." She frowns. "I love the life we have with each other."

"I'm glad, Angel. I just know my schedule is hectic, and I need to learn how to properly balance it all," I say, walking her over to the large-screen TV they have playing videos of dolphins and whales.

The moment we're standing in front of it, a video begins to play images of places that have meant something to us—the bakery where I first saw her, her old front door, where we shared our first kiss, the restaurant we had our first date, and then where we are right now. Chloe looks at the screen then at me as I get down on one knee, opening the ring box.

"Marry me, Chloe. Say you will be my wife."

Her eyes instantly fill with tears as she whispers, "Yes."

Her hand is shaking frantically as I slide the five-carat ring onto her finger. Then I bring it to my mouth and place a kiss on it before standing, bending her over my arm, and kissing her until we're both panting for breath. When I stand us back up, the crowd around us begins to applaud. I look at my angel and smile.

"I CAN'T BELIEVE we're getting married," Chloe says. She holds her hand up to the light coming thought the bedroom window, which makes her ring sparkle.

"You shouldn't have been surprised, Angel."

"I know I shouldn't have, but even now, this seems surreal. I can't believe that you're mine."

My gut twists from knowing that she feels this just like I do.

"I will forever be yours, Angel," I tell her, pulling her hand to my mouth and kissing her fingers.

CHAPTER 6

THE SOUND OF Chloe getting sick has me sitting up in bed. This is the second morning this has occurred. I would assume she's pregnant, but she had her period, so the sickness has me worried.

"Angel," I say quietly, kneeling down beside her and placing a cool rag on the back of her neck. "I'm taking you to the doctor today. I know you said you're fine, but you keep getting sick and I can't stand to see you like this."

"I'm fine," she says sleepily, laying her head in the crook of her arm. "It will pass."

"It's no longer your choice. I'm taking you." I pick her up, carry her to the sink, and help her brush her teeth before helping her get dressed, all while listening to her complain the entire time that she doesn't want to go to the doctor, but I still call and make her appointment.

"YOU'RE OVERREACTING," Chloe repeats for the twentieth time since we arrived at the doctor's office.

I look at her and shake my head. "The doctor will tell me if I'm overreacting or not, and I don't believe I am."

"We should make a bet." She laughs when I look at her and narrow my eyes. "If the doctor says there is nothing wrong and I've just got a bug, like I told you I do, you have to be my slave for twenty-four hours."

"And if I win?"

"I'm at your disposal." She smirks, and I chew the inside of my cheek like I'm debating agreeing to her terms.

"Are you not always at my disposal?" I grin, crowding her against the table.

"I could say no if I wanted to," she breathes as I kiss down the side of her neck to the top of her shirt, imagining having my way with her right now.

"You could say no," I agree, "but you won't." I growl, nipping her skin, and I laugh when she moans my name.

"Can't you just play along?" she huffs, glaring at me when she realizes I'm laughing.

"Fine. If there is nothing wrong, I will do whatever you want. But if I'm right, you have to do whatever I say tonight."

"Deal." She smiles and sticks out her hand, and I give her a shake while laughing at how cute she is.

"You really are feeling better, aren't you?" I question when she begins to laugh.

"I told you I was. I don't know why it happens. I just feel sick sometimes."

"I think you should take a pregnancy test, Angel."

"I already told you I started my period." She frowns.

"Hello," the doctor says, walking into the room, ending the conversation between the two of us.

"How old are you?" I demand; the guy barely looks legal.

"Nolan," Chloe hisses, elbowing me in the ribs.

"The guy hardly looks old enough to drink, let alone practice medicine," I tell her, looking at the doctor, waiting for him to reply.

"I'm actually thirty," he says, smiling at Chloe.

"See? He's old. Now, can we please just get on with this?" Chloe prompts, and the doctor's face falls at the word 'old,' almost making me laugh.

"What seems to be the problem?" he asks, clearing his throat.

"She's been waking up sick," I tell him.

He looks at me then back to Chloe. "Are you pregnant?"

"No! Sheesh." She rolls her eyes.

"Are you sure?" he asks.

"I started my period. So, yes, I'm sure."

"How about we just test you, just in case."

"Fine," she growls.

After snatching the cup he pulled out of the drawer from his hand, she leaves the room, slamming the door. That would be another reason I want to find out if she is pregnant. The past few days, it hasn't taken much to set her off.

"I'll be back with the results," the doctor mutters as he leaves the room.

It only takes five minutes after Chloe gets back for the doctor to step into the room with a piece of paper.

"You're pregnant," the doctor says, walking over to his rolling chair to take a seat, and I freeze in place.

"That's impossible." Chloe looks from the doctor to me. My mouth opens and closes, but not words come out. "Maybe you were right. Maybe he's too immature."

"I did two separate tests to confirm it, and we can do a blood test if that's what you like, but the results will be the same. You're pregnant," he growls then looks at Chloe, who I have pulled into my lap. "A lot of women think they are having their period, but really, they are having what's called implantation bleeding."

"We're pregnant," she says, and I feel her smooth hand on the side of my face. "We're pregnant," she repeats.

My eyes close. I finally have everything I could ever ask for.

"We need to get married," I state.

"We are getting married."

"No, I mean we need to get married *now*." I pause, kissing her lips. "Today."

"Do you want to go to Vegas?" she jokes, but I think that sounds like the perfect idea.

"We'll leave tonight. Mom can plan some kind of party when we get home."

"Nolan, slow down."

"No, we're getting married. I agreed with you before because you wanted to plan the wedding with our mothers, but this is no longer only about you. Now, we have our child growing inside you. Your mother and my mother will just have to get together and plan a party or some shit."

"Plan a party?" she whispers, looking at me like I've lost my mind.

I ignore her and pull out my phone, sending a message to Ricket that tells him to bring the car around. Once we're out of the office with an appointment for a few weeks later and a prescription for prenatal vitamins, we head out of the building.

"Sir, madam," Ricket says.

Chloe rolls her eyes, making Ricket's mouth twitch. She keeps asking him not to call her that, and I believe that, normally, he would stop, but he enjoys ruffling my angel's feathers.

"Ricket, we need to go to the airport. Just call ahead and have the plane readied to leave within the hour for Vegas."

"We're not even going home for clothes?" Chloe asks.

"You can buy clothes in Vegas."

"This is ridiculous."

"This is what I should have done weeks ago. Hell, I should have just taken you to Vegas the first night I met you and married your ass," I say, following her into the back of the car.

"Nolan, you're being crazy."

"Beautiful"—I pull her into my lap and grab her face—"this is not up for debate."

"So we're going to Vegas and getting married without anyone to witness it? Do you have any idea how mad our mothers are going to be?"

"We're not going to argue about this. We're going to Vegas," I tell her.

She presses her lips together and shakes her head. "When your mom hears about this, don't blame me."

"It will be fine." I shrug.

"If you say so," she mutters.

WHEN WE ARRIVE in Vegas, it doesn't take long to get everything in place. Chloe has her dress sent up to the penthouse of the Paris Hotel while we're still in the air, and I take care of a tux for myself. I also have someone brought in to do her hair and makeup along with someone to take photos. Even with this being short notice, I want Chloe to have good memories of this day.

"Who are you speaking to?" I ask her, walking into the bathroom, where there is a group of people around her.

"It's not your mom, if that's what you're asking."

"I know you already did your damage talking to her. Who now? Your mom this time?"

"No, it's Bre. She asked if I could meet her for dinner, but I told her no because my crazy fiancé decided we're getting married today and flew us to Vegas." She rolls her eyes then presses her ear closer to the phone when I give her the signal to hang up.

I told her that I didn't want her speaking to her anymore, but apparently, she is not listening lately. Half the things I say to her go in one ear and out the other. I think she spends her days trying to think up ways to piss me off. I can't even imagine what it will be like now that she is pregnant. As soon as she ends the call, I snatch the phone from her hand.

"I do not want you to talk to her."

"Why?"

"She was one of the women you were with the night you were drugged."

"You don't still believe she had anything to do with that, do you?" she asks.

"I have no way of knowing for sure, so until I have evidence that excludes her, she is not to be trusted."

"What reason would she have to do something like that?" she asks as a frown forms on her lips.

"People do crazy things every day. You never really know the reasoning." I do not want her to live in fear, but the reality of the situation is we don't know who to trust right now, and there is no way I will risk her safety.

I go to her side and spin the chair around, placing a hand on each armrest. "Let's not think about that today." I move a small piece of hair off her forehead with my finger. "Today is about us starting our future and enjoying the fact that you are carrying my child," I declare, watching her face transform and a look of amazement fill her eyes.

"I still can't believe I'm pregnant."

"I can. I think deep down, even after you told me you had started your period, I knew you were pregnant," I say quietly.

"How?" she whispers, leaning towards me with a tender look on her face.

"You've seemed more settled, more at ease, like you're content with where you are."

"I'm with you. How could I not be content?"

"What have you done with my mischievous fiancée?" I grin and she laughs, sitting back in the chair.

"If I acted like everyone else in your life, you would have grown bored with me."

"I doubt that, Angel." I chuckle, kissing her temple before standing to my full height. "I will see you at the altar."

"I'll be there," she murmurs as I turn for the door. "Nolan."

I turn and look at her over my shoulder, watching her swallow then chew on her bottom lip. "What is it, Beautiful?"

SHE LIFTS HER hand before dropping it to her lap, saying quietly, "I wouldn't have you any other way."

Something about those softly spoken words make me feel more powerful than I have ever felt before. A lump forms in my throat and I nod, leaving before I do something pussyish like start crying.

"Son," my father says as soon as I pick up the phone.

"Dad," I reply. I know exactly what's coming. Chloe called my mother on the way to Vegas, and my mother immediately began freaking out. Then she proceeded to call Chloe's mom and add her into the conversation.

"Your mother wanted me to call you to tell you that you are now disowned and cut out of the will."

"Dad, I don't want to sound disrespectful, but I haven't even thought about my inheritance since I turned twenty-five."

"That's exactly what I told her. Regardless, she wanted me to phone you anyway," he says on an exhale.

"Tell Mom that, if she relaxes, I will let her plan the baby shower," I say, hanging up the phone just as my dad prompts, "Pardon?"

It takes approximately thirty seconds for my phone to begin ringing again. I look at the caller ID and smile but press ignore as I head to the elevator. I know my mother, and I know she's in a tizzy over the news that she is going to be a grandma and will forget about the wedding—at least for a little while. Since the moment she met Chloe, she has hinted that we needed to work on making her a grandmother, so now, her wish is coming true.

I arrive at the chapel, and the moment I enter the room, the officiate is at my side, leading me to the altar to wait for Chloe. I never believed I would want to get married again, but Chloe has changed that for me too. The tighter I can tie her to me, the better off I will be. She is my personal brand of kryptonite.

When the music begins to play, I turn towards the door, and my breath instantly stills when Chloe appears. Her dress is all lace, starting at her neck then completely covering her body, including the tops of her hands. The delicate fabric looks like it has been painted onto her, and as much as I love what she is wearing, I can't wait to see what she has on underneath.

When we were in New York, Chloe and my mother were going back and forth about dresses. My mother wanted her to have a certain style of dress, and Chloe wanted something completely different. I stayed out of it unless Chloe asked me to step in. My mother could be opinionated, but Chloe was stubborn as fuck, and if she really wanted something, she would find a way to get it.

Now, seeing her walk to me in a dress I know she picked out, with her hair down and makeup that only enhances her already beautiful face, I am glad Chloe got her dream dress. The officiate says something as she arrives in front of me, but I hear nothing but the beat of my own heart as I pull her closer.

"You look breathtaking," I whisper against the shell of her ear.

Her hands fist into the lapels of my suit as I stand at full height, keeping her so close I can feel the heat of her skin. I'm so entranced by her that the rest of the ceremony is a blur until the moment Chloe takes my hand as the officiate repeats the words I just spoke to her.

I never expected to wear a ring again. I never expected Chloe to have a ring for me to wear, so I'm overwhelmed with emotions as she slides a simple band onto my finger. I don't even wait for his permission to kiss the bride. As soon as her eyes travel from the ring that is now on my finger up to lock with my eyes, I wrap a hand around her waist, bend her back over my arm, and take her mouth in a deep kiss.

"Thank you, Angel," I whisper against her mouth.

"For what?" she whispers back, looking up into my eyes. The look in hers is so vulnerable and trusting that I know I have been given the greatest gift anyone could ever receive.

"You," I grunt, overwhelmed with emotion as I pick her up and carry her to the elevator, ignoring the startled look from the chapel staff.

CHAPTER 7

As soon as I get the door to the suite open, I step through and kick it closed behind us, causing Chloe to laugh.

"How much do you love this dress?" I ask her, tossing her onto the bed. Then I quickly strip off my jacket and shirt before crawling on top of her.

"It was expensive," she moans as my hand travels up her inner thigh then up the center of her pussy, feeling that the material of her panties is already soaked through.

"I could buy a million of these dresses. I just want to know how much you love it before I rip it off you."

Her eyes close and her lips part as my fingers slide into the side of her panties. "I love it," she breathes, making me smile.

"You love the dress or me touching your pussy, Angel?" I ask, and her hips shift.

It takes a moment for her to come back to herself, but when she does, her head lifts and our eyes lock.

"Both," she moans, pressing her hips down, causing my fingers to slide into her.

"You better take it off then," I growl, slowly my fingers move in and out of her, my thumb circling her clit.

"Stop," she cries, and I shake my head, lift the front of her dress up, lower my face, and suck her pussy through the material of her panties.

"Take it off, Angel," I snarl, biting the lips of her pussy.

"I can't when you're doing that!" she screams.

I slow down and lift up slightly as her shaky hands begin to shift her dress up and then pause.

"The back is buttoned," she hisses.

"Interesting," I mutter, flipping her to her stomach then climbing back between her legs.

Her hands go to the bed, putting her on all fours in front of me as I slowly begin unbuttoning her dress from the back of her neck down to her hips. As I carefully slide the fabric down her shoulders, I expose a lace bra the exact color of her flawless skin.

I run a finger from the back of her neck down to her lower back then back up again to trace the edge of the material before pulling her up with a hand under her waist so that she is kneeling in front of me. Her head leans back against my shoulder as her hands cover mine. It slides her dress off her body then back up to cup her breasts, twisting her nipples through the lacy material.

"This is pretty," I whisper against her neck, looking down over her shoulder at her bra before pulling the straps down, exposing her breasts and watching as her already hard nipples become harder when they hit the cold air of the room.

"Thank you." She smiles, lifting her hands up and behind her head to wrap around my neck.

"You're welcome." I smirk, gliding my hand down her stomach, into her panties, and through the lips of her pussy before slipping them inside her and using my fingers to pull her hips back. I press my hips towards her ass, my cock settling between her cheeks through the material of her panties and my dress slacks. "You're soaked, Angel," I tell her as I fuck into her pussy hard with my fingers. "Do you want to come?" I question, biting her shoulder, neck, and then her ear.

"Yes," she says shakily.

"Give me your hand," I demand, and she slowly lowers one hand down. I grab her wrist, intertwining our fingers before slipping our hands between her legs.

"Nolan," she whispers, sounding unsure.

"Shhhh, Angel. Just feel," I tell her, nipping her jaw.

Her head turns towards me, and I shove my tongue into her mouth while pushing her fingers inside her pussy. Her thighs begin to shake as I use my fingers and hand to control the pace. Then I pull my mouth from hers. Her eyes are at half-mast, her lips swollen and pink.

"Do you feel that, how wet you are?" I ask, pulling her fingers out and bringing them to her mouth. "Open," I tell her, and her lips part as I press her fingers into her mouth. "You taste that? You taste more amazing than anything I have ever eaten in my life and sweeter than the sweetest honey," I say, pulling her hand away and covering her mouth with mine as I pump our fingers into her again, her cries filling my mouth as her pussy convulses.

"Oh, God," she whimpers as her pussy soaks my hand and her body slumps forward.

I gently lay her down and move so I can slip the dress off her completely before taking off the rest of my clothes. Once I'm undressed, I crawl back up onto the bed. She lifts her hips, and then she pulls her panties down, dragging them her legs before tossing them at me and opening her thighs, showing me the evidence of her arousal.

My girl has become so brave. It seems like just yesterday I popped her cherry.

I lift her ass to sit on my thighs and open the lips of her pussy with one hand, wrapping the other around my width, and groan. I'm in so much pain. My balls are so tight that I know I won't last long, but the night is young. I also know she will not be getting much sleep tonight.

"Easy, baby," I tell her as she tries to lift her hips so the head of my cock slides an inch inside.

I grab her hands and pull her up, lowering my hips before raising them slowly. There is nothing better than feeling the wetness of her pussy as she uses her inner muscles to grip my cock.

"You're so fucking hot, baby. Fuck, your pussy feels like it's on fire," I groan, lowering my head so I can watch myself disappear into her heat.

"Nolan," she cries, and her hands go to my shoulders, where her nails dig into my skin.

I lower her back onto the bed and fuck her, making sure I don't go as deep as I normally would.

"Please," she begs as I slow down.

"No, Angel, we need to be careful."

"No, harder." She claws at my back and begins to thrash under me.

I grab her hands and hold them next to her head so I can control her. "Calm down," I snarl, rolling my hips towards hers, feeling my length drag along her inner walls as she ripples around me.

"Nolan."

"I'm here, Beautiful," I whisper into her ear, slowing my thrusts and pressing kisses to the skin of her neck, cheek, and mouth. Then I release her wrists and hold her face between my hands while resting on my elbows. As I look into her eyes, I remember I now own her in the eyes of God and the law. She is mine, now and forever.

How the fuck I got so lucky, I have no idea, but knowing who she is to me, what she means to our future, has my thrusts going deeper and harder. Her head goes tilts and her back arches off the bed as her fingers scrape down my skin, leaving marks. Her pussy begins to ripple, and I thrust two more times before bottoming out deep inside her.

"Fuck," I roar, coming hard. My muscles relax and I slump forward, careful not to put pressure onto her lower stomach.

"I love you," she whispers, and I gaze into her eyes. The love I see shining back at me solidifies that, as much as I own her, she owns me, and I wouldn't have it any other way.

"Sleep, Angel," I tell her, kissing her forehead then rolling to my side and pulling her into my arms.

When her breathing evens out, I turn off the lights and pick up my cell phone from the bedside table. The first thing I see is a message from my mom.

"You told her I'm pregnant?" is groggily whispered.

I look down at Chloe and fight back my smile when I see her glaring at me by the light from the phone.

"Oh my God!" she yells, grabbing the phone from my hand. "She called my mom!" she cries, sitting up in bed and looking at me over her shoulder.

I put my hands behind my head and cross my ankles, smiling. "I had to give her something. She was upset about the wedding."

"So you told her I was pregnant? Do you realize what you've done? My mom and your mom are going to freak out."

"They will be fine. Just let them plan the baby shower."

"Let them plan the baby shower," she mumbles, staring at the phone.

"Angel, it's fine. Don't worry."

"Don't worry?" she mutters under her breath.

I sit up and kiss her shoulder. "It will be okay," I tell her, wrapping a hand around her waist.

"I think you're delusional." She shakes her head, handing me back my phone.

"I can't believe you told them that I'm pregnant just so they would not freak out on you."

"That is not why. I just wanted them to know. That way, they would have something else to look forward to."

"Our mothers called me every day to talk about the wedding. Do you know what they are going to do now that they know I'm having a baby?"

"They are excited."

"Yes, and now, I'll never get a break 'cause they are going to call or come over. I wouldn't be surprised if my mom talks my dad into buying an RV so she can stay close…like 'our driveway' close," she says, flopping back onto the bed.

"Your parents are not living in our driveway." I frown.

"If you say so. They are probably already on their way to New York now."

"No," I deny, glaring at her.

"Hey, it's not my fault you have a big mouth. Be mad at yourself. I mean, for all I know, your parents are moving in as well."

"Our parents are not living with us."

"Okay," she mutters, and I see a smile twitch her cheek.

"Maybe we should just build onto the house and have both

our parents move in. We do have plenty of land," I suggest.

"What?" she shrieks, making me chuckle. "That's not funny." She rolls her eyes, and I pull her down to me, tucking her head under my chin.

"Everything will be okay." I press a kiss to the top of her head.

"I know." She yawns, and I pull the blanket up over us.

Nothing matters anymore but us, and I know we will always be okay.

"Mom, calm down. What happened?" I ask, pulling my phone from my ear slightly so I can understand her better.

"Chloe!" she cries, and my stomach drops.

"What happened to Chloe?"

"She was almost run over and fell. We called an ambulance."

"What do you mean 'she was almost run over'?" I growl.

"We were leaving the baby store and she was getting into the car when a motorcycle came down the sidewalk and almost ran her over. She got out of the way, but she fell and hit her head against a parking meter."

"Where is she now?"

"In the ambulance."

"Jesus. Where are you exactly?" I roar as I run out of my office.

We haven't even been home for a week. Since we've been back, our mothers have been keeping her busy with shopping and constant nagging about what is good for her and the baby. I was planning to go home tonight and force everyone out of our house so that I could get some alone time with Chloe, where we could just enjoy the fact that she's pregnant. Life has been so consuming that I forgot Chloe was in danger and we have something to be concerned about.

"We're at Bu and the Duck, near Church Street."

"I'm on my way!" I shout into the phone as I head out of the lobby.

Just as I'm about to hail a cab, Ricket pulls around the corner in my car. I open up the backdoor and hop in.

"I need to get to Bu and the Duck on Church Street."

"I know, sir," Ricket says, and I pull of my suit jacket, tossing it across the back seat.

"How did this happen?"

"I don't know, sir. I found out when her mother called me."

"Her mom called you?" I ask, looking at him in the rearview mirror.

His eyes connect with mine as he nods before looking back at the road. "She said you would need to be picked up and where they were at."

"Did she say anything else?"

"No, sir. She was distraught."

"Yeah," I mumble, looking out the window.

It takes less time than normal to make it across town. Once we reach the block my mom told me they were at, I see cop cars and a crying Chloe sitting in the open door of an ambulance. I don't even wait for the car to come to a complete stop before I jump out and head straight for her. When I'm almost at her side, a police officer steps in front of me and nearly gets punched in the face as I try to get around him.

"This is her husband," my mom says as I fight with the cop to get by.

The cop looks at her and releases the hold he has on my upper arm, letting me get to Chloe.

"Nolan!" she gasps through tears.

"I'm here, Angel." I wrap my arms around her, kissing the white bandage on her forehead.

"Who called you? I told them not to call you." She shakes her head, pulling back to look up into my eyes.

"Excuse me?"

"I didn't want you to worry. I didn't want you to have to leave work."

"Beautiful, do you know the kind of trouble you would be in if I would have found out about what happened later instead of right now? You never keep anything from me, especially if that something has to do with you."

"I'm fine, and you worry too much."

"You were almost run over. You have a cut on your forehead, fell, and now have tears streaming down your cheeks and you don't think I have a reason to worry?" I bark, making her jump.

"I know it sounds bad," she mumbles, making a growl vibrate my chest.

"It not only sounds bad, but *is* bad, Angel. Now, tell me. Have they made sure the baby is okay?"

"The baby is fine. I didn't fall hard."

"Chloe, I'm beginning to wonder if you understand what the fuck happened."

"I know exactly what happened. I was walking out of the store when a stupid delivery bike almost ran me over. I jumped out of the way and tripped, hitting my head on one of the meters."

"You don't find it odd that a motorcycle was driving on a sidewalk of one of the nicest streets in Manhattan?"

"I don't know." She shrugs and smiles at the EMT, making

me growl at him, which causes him to jump back and me to get hit in the chest.

"This is not a joke, Chloe. You could have been seriously hurt—or worse."

"I know it's not a joke, but I don't think you're right about this. I think it was an accident. I mean, how would anyone even know where to find me?"

That's what I'm going to find out. None of this was by chance. There had to be a reason all of this is happening now.

"I will figure it out, but until then, you're not to go out unless I'm with you."

"I would like to remind you that I didn't want to go out in the first place, but our mothers insisted I find a christening gown." She lifts her hands before dropping them to her side. "I didn't even know we are Catholic," she complains, making me smile despite the situation and kiss her head.

"We're not Catholic—well, not practicing, anyways. But Mom was baptized, and so was I, so she just wants to keep the tradition."

"I think our moms need a hobby that doesn't include me."

"They are excited about the baby."

"I know." She leans her head on my shoulder as we watch the police talk to our mothers while Bernard stands near them, listening to the details of what occurred.

I make eye contact with Bernard and nod when he shakes his head. I can tell that he doesn't believe this was an accident either.

CHAPTER 8

"Who's on the phone?" I ask Chloe, walking into the bedroom, where she is sitting up on the side of the bed with the phone to her ear while she paints her toenails some strange purple color.

"Bre called to see if I was okay," she says, leaning her head back and accepting my kiss.

"What did I tell you about speaking to her" I ask.

She presses her lips together then frowns and pulls the phone from her ear, setting it down on the bed next to her hip.

"What's wrong?"

"She hung up." She shrugs and begins painting again.

"Good," I mutter, looking down at the phone and seeing that the image on the screen is a picture of Bre that pops up when she calls. The longer I look at the picture, the more something in the back of my head keeps niggling me. I know her from somewhere, but I just cannot place where. I shake off the feeling and head for the shower.

My guys are working on getting the security tapes from what happened this afternoon. Hopefully, they will have something for me before too long. I want all of this shit taken care of before

Chloe has our child. There is no fucking way I will be able to work if I think for even one moment my family is in danger.

"WHAT'S THIS?" I ask as I walk into my living room.

Four heads turn my way, and I know that Chloe is going to get her ass spanked tonight for disobeying me again when one of the heads that turns towards me is Bre's.

"Our moms were here going over the plans for the nursery and Bre stopped by to bring me flowers, and when she saw what we were doing, she asked to see the plans," Chloe says as her eyes plead with me to understand.

But all I can think about is the woman in front of me and the familiar way she looks. My mind keeps nagging at me to remember, but for some reason, there is a block. The idea of her knowing anything about the room that my child will sleep in makes me feel like I could kill.

I look at Chloe and nod towards the kitchen. She bites her lip but gets up from where she's sitting on the floor and heads in that direction. I give her a few moments before following behind her. When I reach the kitchen, Chloe is standing near the sink, her eyes on the doorway, and she looks away as soon as our eyes connect.

"What did I tell you about Bre?" I growl, stepping towards her.

"Be reasonable, Nolan," she pleads, looking back at me.

"What did I tell you, Chloe?"

Her face falls at the sound of her name. I never her call her by her name; I have always called her Angel or Beautiful. But she has pushed me too far.

"I don't understand why you have such a problem with her."

"I told you already I do not trust her. I also explained that, once I find out what is going on with you, and if she has been cleared and proven to be innocent, you can resume your friendship."

"She's really nice. If you just give her a chance, you will see that."

I shake my head no. "People believed that some of the most notorious mass murders in history were nice, Chloe. So please forgive me if I don't buy it."

"You're insane," she hisses.

"Get rid of her or I will," I snarl, pointing towards the door of the kitchen.

"Fine." She stomps out of the kitchen.

I follow a few steps behind her into the living room. When I walk around the corner, Chloe is talking to our mothers and Bre is nowhere in sight.

"Are you happy now?" Chloe asks, turning to look at me. "She left."

"Good." I shrug.

My mother looks at me like she's going to say something, but I hold up my hand.

"Chloe is in danger, and until I know who is trying to hurt her, everyone is a suspect."

"Darling," my mother stammers, putting a hand over her heart.

"No. This is not up for discussion. And know that if you do anything to put her in danger and she goes along with it, I will be spanking her ass for it."

"Oh my," Chloe's mother mutters as Chloe's eyes light with fire.

"Now, I have work to do. Please stay out of trouble," I tell them before leaving the room and heading towards my office.

In the back of my head, all I can think about is Bre—something about her is setting off red flags. I know I may seem a bit harsh right now, but this is about keeping my woman and unborn child safe, and I will do whatever is necessary to see to that.

"YOU'RE SURE ABOUT this?" I ask Bernard while going through the stack of pictures he just handed to me.

"One hundred percent certain," he says as I come across a picture of my ex-wife with Bre.

It took some time for it to click, but after a few days, I got it. I realized who Bre really was. Plastic surgery had changed her appearance, but her eyes were still the same.

Breanne's were just like my ex's—her older sister's—cold and distant. She had a way of looking at you that made you feel like she was looking right through you.

"Tell me what the plan is," I say, leaning back in my chair and setting the pictures down on the top of my desk.

"Hear me out before you say anything." He sits down.

"If your idea has anything to do with Chloe, the answer is no."

"Hear me out."

"No." I slam my hand down on the top of my desk.

"I want to build the best case possible," he says calmly.

"Do that without risking Chloe in the process," I snarl, the idea of Chloe being in danger making my blood boil.

"I would never let anything happen to Chloe." He shakes his head, running a hand through his hair.

"I know *I* would never let anything happen to Chloe." I point a finger at myself. "And I refuse to put her in harm's way, so figure something else out."

"I will figure something else out," he says.

I nod and watch as he walks away. Then I pick up my phone and look at the clock on the wall.

"Shit," I mutter, picking up my phone. "Hello."

"Darling, you need to come home," my mother says in a tone I have not heard from her since I was thirteen and my dog got run over.

"What is it?"

"Just come home," she whispers before the phone goes dead.

I rush out of my office and out of the building, where Ricket is waiting for me.

"What happened?" I roar.

He shakes his head and opens the door to the car. I try to call everyone on the ride home, but no one is available. When we finally pull up to the estate, I see that there are at least ten police cruisers out front. I don't even wait for the car to come to a complete stop before I'm out running to Chloe.

"What happened?" I demand from the officer while pulling Chloe into my arms, breathing in her scent.

"The two women in the back of the squad car over there tried to kidnap her," the officer says.

I follow his eyes to a police car that is parked near the entrance to our home. Lynda and Breanne are both handcuffed and sitting in the back of a squad car. I push Chloe slightly away and begin checking her over, making sure she was not harmed. Once I see that she is okay, I pull her back towards my chest.

"Are you okay?"

"I'm fine. Bre told me that she wanted to go out for lunch. I told her that I couldn't. Then she told me she had something for the baby in her car and to walk her out. I…" She pauses. "I just got a weird feeling. So I told her I would get it from her another time, and that's when the other woman pushed into the house. Then Bernard and a few other guys showed up," she says quietly.

I shudder at the idea of what could have happened. Then I look around the crowd for Bernard and give him a chin lift.

It takes about an hour for the police to leave after getting statements from everyone, and I have Chloe's mother and mine take Chloe inside while I talk to Bernard. It seems that he tracked down my ex-wife and her sister in a small, one-bedroom apartment in SOHO. When they were able to enter their apartment, they realized the extent of their delusion. The two of them had devoted their lives to trying to hurt me.

From what they were able to gather, Lynda and Breanne had planned for me to meet Breanne and begin a relationship with her. They believed I would marry her at some point, and then their plan was to have me murdered and collect the money from my life insurance. When they realized I was already taken, they formed a new plan to use my devotion to Chloe against me.

They drugged Chloe and were going to try to set it up to make it look like she had been cheating on me with her high school boyfriend. When that didn't work, they were planning on making it look like Chloe had moved out on me, and they sent Chloe the e-mail with the pictures of me in Japan, planning on Chloe seeing them and ignoring my calls. All of their plans were being foiled, and when Chloe told Bre that we'd gotten married, that sent my ex over the edge and she tried to run Chloe over.

After Bernard and everyone leaves, I find Chloe in the library, standing in front of one of the windows, looking out over the estate. I walk to her.

"They are really insane," she whispers as I reach her side.

I wrap an arm around her shoulders, watching as Bernard pulls away. "They are, and they are both going away for a very long time."

"I hate that Bre did this," she whispers.

I'm not one to condone hitting women, but I could choke the shit out of that bitch for making my beautiful angel this upset, for coming into her life, pretending to be her friend, and then using her like she did.

"I'm sorry, Angel."

"Me too," she says, stepping out of my hold and walking out of the room.

I watch her go, knowing I will only give her a little time to get over what happened. I do not want her to dwell on this shit—not when we have so much to be happy about.

"GET UP," I tell Chloe as I walk into the bedroom.

"For what?" she asks, looking at me from over the top of her Kindle, not moving.

"You're not going to lie around and pout all day. Now, get up."

"I'm not pouting." She frowns.

I shake my head, walk over to her, rip the Kindle out of her hand, and toss it onto a chair across the room.

"Hey! I was reading that," she complains, crossing her arms over her chest and glaring at me.

"I don't know what happened to my submissive little Angel,

but I'm telling you now—what you're going to be doing is getting undressed, getting on your knees, opening that pretty mouth of yours, and sucking my cock until I tell you to stop. Then, if you're good, I will eat your little pussy until you come," I growl, pulling her out of bed. "When I've had my fill of your taste, you're going to climb up on my cock and ride me until we both come."

"Nolan," she hisses as I rip her shirt off over her head.

"No." I turn her around, bend her over the bed, and spank her ass with three hard swats before bending over her and growling in her ear, "Enough." Then I move my hips so my cock is sitting in the crook of her ass. Using one hand to free up her pants, I pull them down around her thighs and then slide my hand between her legs, feeling her arousal coat my fingers. "You're so wet, Angel," I tell her, sucking my fingers into my mouth. Then I unbuckle my pants, freeing myself before sliding just the tip inside her. "Do you want me to fuck you?" I groan, sliding in a little deeper.

"Yes," she breathes, trying to press back against me.

"Then do what I tell you."

I press into her balls-deep then pull out slowly, feeling my length slide along her inner walls. Once I slide out completely, I fight the urge to slide back in and quickly help remove the rest of her clothing. Then I pull one of the pillows from the bed before setting it at my feet and helping her to her knees in front of me. As soon as her knees touch the pillow, her eyes meet mine and her mouth opens.

"Lick it," I command.

She starts at the head then works her way down my shaft to the base until my cock is halfway down her throat. Her hands travel up my thighs, and one wraps around the base. She begins twisting it, bobbing her head. I start to feel the tingle in the bottom of my spine.

"Easy, Angel," I groan, not ready to come.

She releases me on a pop, and I help her stand then position her as I had her earlier, leaning over the side of the bed with the fat lips of her pussy peeking at me from between her legs. I fall to my knees behind her, wrap my hands around her thighs, and bury my face between her legs, probing her entrance with my tongue then sucking her clit into my mouth.

Her body starts bucking against my face and her loud moans begin to fill the room. I move my hands and spread her pussy open farther, paying close attention to her clit, fluttering my tongue against it until she begins to flood my mouth with her sweet juices while her nails dig into my arms and her toes raise her up off the floor.

I slow down and ease her out of her orgasm before helping her stand up and turn to face me. When I look up at her, her eyes are clouded with desire. I take a breath then place a kiss above her pubic bone. Then on her lower stomach, where the life we created together is growing. I stand and get on the bed, helping her up and over me with her thighs straddling my hips. As soon as she is in position, the look in her eyes changes and she sinks down on me until the tip of my cock touches her cervix.

She leans forward, her hands holding on to my shoulder as her hips rise and fall. I pull her face down to mine, biting her bottom lip then the top, leaning back to look at her as her eyes close to half-mast and her hips start to move quicker. My hands travel down her hair and back to her ass, holding one cheek in each palm, lifting and dropping her onto me as her pussy begins to milk my come from my cock, the fluttering drawing my orgasm to the surface.

Her scream and my roar travel through the air at the same time that her body slumps forward and my head bends back into the pillow. It takes a few moments to catch my breath and for my heart beat to go back to normal, but when it does, I use my fingers under her chin to lift her face up towards mine.

"Love you, Angel," I say, and her face goes soft. "From this day forward, we're just going to enjoy life. I know what happened is horrible, but we have too much to live for."

"You're right," she says as her face goes even softer.

I pull her back down onto me, tucking her head under my chin, where she fits perfectly. No matter what happened in my past or what I have gone through, having this with her now makes all those struggles worth it.

EPILOGUE

"I CAN'T SEE my feet." Chloe laughs as I open the glass shower door. "There is no way I can shave my legs." She shakes her head, sitting down on the marble bench that is built into the shower wall.

"You look beautiful," I insist as I run my fingers through her hair, gently tilting her head back.

"You love me, so you have to say I look beautiful." She sighs, opening her eyes and looking up at me.

"I do love you, but you are beautiful as well. I love seeing you pregnant with my children."

"I know," she mutters, rolling her eyes. "I learned that after the first three kids."

"You have begged for them each time," I tell her, smirking.

"I told you before. If we're in the moment, it doesn't count."

She laughs as I mimic her screaming for me to give her my seed.

"Mommy!" our daughter yells, breaking the moment.

I sigh and close my eyes. I wanted nothing more than to finally get a piece of Chloe. I thought we had finally snuck away, but as usual, our kids have perfect timing.

"Your mom comes into town tonight, so you better plan on not sleeping for the next twenty-four hours."

"Nolan."

"No." I shake my head and pull her closer, lowering my mouth over one of her nipples. "I need you." I lick around her nipple before biting down. "I need to be inside you."

"You had me this morning."

"That was only me getting rid of my morning wood. That doesn't count. You owe me," I tell her and smile when she begins to laugh.

"You're obsessed."

She is not wrong. I have been obsessed with her from the moment I met her, and nothing has changed. Even after five years, three kids, and another one on the way, we're still inseparable, and I want her more now than ever.

What can I say? I have a beautiful wife.

Liability **– Book 2 of the ALFHA LAW Series**

Carter doesn't know what to expect when he is forced to work with the Alfha Law Firm on a case, but he never expects to fall for the boss's granddaughter.

OTHER BOOKS BY THIS AUTHOR

The Until Series
Until November – NOW AVAILABLE
Until Trevor – NOW AVAILABLE
Until Lilly – NOW AVAILABLE
Until Nico – NOW AVAILABLE
Second Chance Holiday – NOW AVAILABLE

Underground Kings Series
Assumption – NOW AVAILABLE
Obligation – COMING SOON
Distraction – COMING SOON

Alpha Law
Justified – NOW AVAILABLE
Liability – COMING SOON
Verdict – COMING SOON

ABOUT THE AUTHOR

NEW YORK TIMES & USA TODAY BESTSELLING AUTHOR Aurora Rose Reynolds started writing so that the over the top alpha men that lived in her head would leave her alone. When she's not writing or reading she spends her days with her very own real life alpha who loves her as much as the men in her books love their women and their Great Dane Blue that always keeps her on her toes.

For more information on books that are in the works or just to say hello, follow me on Facebook:
www.facebook.com/pages/Aurora-Rose-Reynolds/474845965932269

Goodreads:
www.goodreads.com/author/show/7215619.Aurora_Rose_Reynolds

Twitter:
@Auroraroser

E-mail Aurora she would love to hear from you:
Auroraroser@gmail.com

Cover Designer

Sara Eirew

www.saraeirew.com

Cover models

Dave Santa Lucia – Fitness Model

www.facebook.com/davesantaluciafitnessmodel

e-mail – david.f.santalucia@gmail.com

Rachael Baltes-Model

www.facebook.com/Rachael.Baltes.Model

e-mail – Rachael.baltes@gmail.com

ACKNOWLEDGMENT

First I want to give thanks to God without him none of this would be possible.

Second I want to thank my husband for always being so supportive and cheering me on even when I want to throw in the towel. To my editors Kayla, You know I adore you woman. Thank you for always knowing exactly what I'm trying to say. Missy thank you for all your insightfulness and Michelle thank you for your keen eye you each work so hard and I'm so thankful for that.

Thank you to my cover designer and friend Sara Eirew your design and photography skills are unbelievable and I will shout that from the rooftops.

Thank you David Santa Lucia and Rachael Baltes you are both amazing and thank you for allowing me to have you on my book cover.

Thank you to TRSOR you girls are always so hard working I will forever be thankful for everything you do.

To my Beta's I think I have said it a million time's but I couldn't ask for better, thank you all so much for always encouraging me. Aurora's Roses I wish I could hug each and ever one of you. I wish you could all know how much you all brighten my days. To every Blog and reader thank you for taking the time to read and share my books. And to my FBGM girls I'm always grateful to be on this journey with each of you.

XOXO
Aurora

*To my good buy
Warmest wishes
Jack Phillips*

A Strange Encounter at Little Hubery
By
Jack C. Phillips

Camelot Publishing Company

A Strange Encounter at Little Hubery
Copyright © 2014 by Jack C. Phillips
All rights reserved. Printed in the United States and the United Kingdom.
No part of this book may be used or reproduced in any manner whatsoever without written permission except in the case of brief quotations embodied in critical articles and reviews.

In Loving Memory of My Mother
Doreen Phillips

Also for my boys
Scott, Josh, Mason & Bernardo

Nothing - but nothing - is quite as atmospheric as a railway: a village's link with the outside world, a country station where an only son set off for war, a bustling terminus where the grand and the bland go about their travels. So it follows that it throws up ghosts - of journeys past, of lovers gone, of children emigrated, of work done, and of prisoners returned.

Hustle, toil, noise, steam, smoke, joy, despair, honeymoons, deaths – all are entwined and encompassed by railways, on lines both extant and extinct...

Chris Bates 1989
Excerpted from the Foreword to
Railway Ghosts & Phantoms

Acknowledgments

My continuing appreciation to Camelot, particularly Mica Rossi, whose support is invaluable, whose belief is incredible and whose friendship is inimitable.

Thank you to the wonderfully talented Chris Bates for allowing us the use of what must be one of the most beautifully worded forewords ever.

This book goes out to my beloved Mother, Doreen Phillips, whose presence made this world a better place and whose absence is keenly felt by all who knew and loved her.

Foreword

This is the second of Jack Phillips' books that I have had the privilege of reading, editing, and producing. When he asked me to write this, I wasn't sure I should, mainly because I wrote the foreword for his last book and thought it might be nice to let someone else have a crack at it. But the more I thought about it, the more I wanted to have a say for this book, too. Because although this one is completely different, I love it every bit as much as I did the other.

With his first book, *No. 41 Burlington Road*, Phillips took us on a tour of an unassuming British neighborhood and uncovered the secrets hidden within its homes, from attic to basement. *A Strange Encounter at Little Hubery* takes us on a tour of a different kind.

The author's love of trains is evident in every chapter, and woven skillfully into the narrative are snippets of history about the railway lines and rural stations that disappeared decades ago. Across the north Yorkshire moors to a time just far enough into the past to have been forgotten by many, Phillips gathers together a group of unlikely characters and thrusts them into the middle of a situation and set of circumstances guaranteed to bring out either the best in them, or the worst in them.

This book is full of the stuff of ghost tales from days gone by, a bit spooky and just enough creepy to satisfy the desire for a good shiver. Its lush descriptions and quirky characters are merely the icing on this cake. Whether you are a lover of trains or not, Phillips' ability to tell a compelling tale will draw you in, and if you were not a fan of all things railway at the beginning, you will be by the end of the story. I guarantee you will want to make yourself a cup of something warm, light the fire, and curl up in your easy chair for a long, quiet evening.

Mica Rossi
2014

Prologue

The man leant against the parapet and straightened his tie. The view from bridge three-sixty-one allowed him to see for miles around, but the woodland, coastline and untamed natural beauty of the surrounding moorland held no charm for him. Not today.

It had been another hot day and the sun was setting on the horizon, weaving braids of fiery red across the sky. The man wiped beads of perspiration from his forehead and looked at his fob-watch. Only another ten minutes to go and then it would all be over. He thought of his fiancée and how he'd let her down. He hoped that she'd understand and that one day she'd be able to forgive him.

Five minutes now and his mouth felt parched. His hands were shaking and his vision hazy. He thought he could hear the approaching engine, the York express, a 0-6-0 Saddle tank locomotive pulling four coaches. He heard the low whistle down the line and the faint humming of the vibrating track. He knew the engine was building up a good head of steam as it worked hard against the grade, and he heard the familiarly comforting rhythmical clunk of the side irons. He fancied he could smell the burning fuel, just whispers of smoke on the wind's breath. And then he saw her on the horizon, emerging from the tunnel like a beautiful armoured goddess of war. A testament to power and ingenuity, her paintwork gleaming in the bright sunlight. A vision of splendour shimmering and wavering in the incandescent heat.

Trembling now, he climbed over and onto the narrow ledge, the roar becoming deafening as the train approached.

'Please God, forgive me!' he cried out in anguish. He paused for a second as he thought he heard the sweetest of voices calling out his name, and he looked around him blindly, his eyes blurred with tears. The train was but a few feet away and he knew the voice was in his head, that he would never again hear his beloved Elizabeth.

But Elizabeth was calling him…Elizabeth was there. She'd arrived at the bridge just in time to see her husband-to-be throw himself off

A Strange Encounter at Little Hubery

the ledge and into the path of the oncoming train.

Chapter One - Then

Little Hubery station was opened in eighteen-seventy-two by the Malton to Redcar branch of the London and North Eastern Railway Company to satisfy demand for customers travelling south to the market towns of Pickering and Helmsley, or North towards Middlesbrough.

A goods line had long since run along the outskirts of the hamlet known as Little Hubery, but the nearest passenger embarkation point had been Clarings Brook Halt, (actually a decent sized station despite its name) a little over nine mile away. Shearing's Vale, a larger station another twelve mile northwest served goods and passengers and had lines bearing east to Whitby and the coast and west toward Darlington and Scotch Corner, as well as joining Little Hubery with stations further north.

Little Hubery lay with its back to open moorland, close enough to the coast to be able

A Strange Encounter at Little Hubery

to taste the salt in the air, and was totally exposed to the winds that swept off the North Sea and howled across the vast empty landscape. It was a quiet, isolated spot, the kind of place people regularly passed through on the train but rarely stopped off at. Sometimes a train would terminate there, leaving passengers to wait for the next one along to Shearing's Vale, but this was uncommon, and so Little Hubery remained a peaceful out-post.

The station itself was opened August seventeenth, eighteen-seventy-two by the then Mayor of Scarborough. It consisted of a waiting room with booking office, a two-roomed staff office and a small toilet block further down the platform. The opposite down platform housed a stone shelter, behind which were a couple of sheds, with a small siding and goods loop further down the line. Behind the sheds were a river, the stationmaster's house, and then open moorland.

It was built of local stone on two raised island platforms with a connecting bridge and was situated off a small side road. The salty sea air and the vulnerable moorland position had given the station an aged, weathered look, and the offices and waiting room remained cool during summer months and provided a cosy refuge for passengers travelling in colder weather.

Stationmaster Arthur McLaren had worked at Little Hubery since nineteen-twenty-three, inheriting the title from his late father Albert, who had retired in twenty-five. He was a proud man and like many railway workers of his time, he was a trusted and committed employee, married to his job and entirely dependable. Arthur, a booking office clerk, two porter-signalmen and a cleaner accounted for the entire staff at Little Hubery at that time.

Being isolated as it was and wearing its weathered countenance, Little Hubery station, abandoned and locked up late at night, was the subject of many a tale from superstitious townsfolk, who gathered around the inglenook in the village inn on cold winter's nights. Some of them claimed, albeit not within earshot of Arthur, that old Albert McLaren, the second and longest-serving stationmaster at Little Hubery, had never left and still presided over the running of the station, even in death.

A Strange Encounter at Little Hubery

Arthur, a level-headed no nonsense kind of fellow, scoffed at ridiculous tales of hauntings in general. He'd witnessed nothing in his many years serving as stationmaster or as clerk before it, and what his eye didn't see, so his mind refused to believe in. Although he'd be the first to admit that the station did seem more than a little creepy on dark, winter nights when the wind howled across the moor, bringing with it vague whisperings from disembodied voices. On nights such as these the flickering gaslights exaggerated rather than eliminated the dark nooks and shadowy corners of the station buildings, allowing imaginations to run wild. But Hubery was his station, it was what it was, and it was hard to imagine that any station in such a lonely, isolated spot would not attract tales of a similar nature.

Chapter Two

The stationmaster's bones creaked as he rose from his chair. He opened the door from his office and stepped outside onto the platform in good time to see the two-thirty express train to York thundering through the station.

'Hmm,' he murmured, snapping shut his fob-watch in satisfaction. 'Not a minute before time, not a second after.'

He looked up at the clouds that hung ominously over the station. It had been threatening rain all day, and the wind had been getting up for the last couple of hours.

'We're in for a belter of a storm,' he said to himself, trying not to give in to the feelings of despondency that arose from time to time when working in an isolated moorland spot. He thought of the mountain of paperwork he had to get through that afternoon and how a good fire,

A Strange Encounter at Little Hubery

a cup of tea and Alistair Cook on the wireless would improve his mood

The stationmaster nodded to a couple of passengers who had just emerged from the booking office, presumably waiting for the two-forty-five to Redcar.

Around him the moorland was eerily quiet, only a distant rumble of thunder breaking the peaceful repose. From somewhere far off came the lonely cry of a hawk out on the moor, and the first few drops of rain caught on the wind and settled on his nose and eyelashes. Another peal of thunder, closer this time and the stationmaster couldn't suppress a shudder.

The couple walked arm in arm along to the other end of the platform. The young man said something and the girl giggled. I really don't like the look of those clouds, thought the stationmaster as he opened the waiting room door. After checking on Percy, his clerk, he made for his office and switched on his wireless, trying hard to combat the feelings of unease that were gaining momentum as the day went on.

Chapter Three

Sir Gregory Barnes, knighted for services to the bar and recently retired, hated train journeys. All the fuss and bother, the dirty, overcrowded stations, and as for the trains themselves! Travelling shoulder to shoulder across the length and breadth of the countryside with people from all walks of life, it really was a tiresome mode of transport and one quite unsuitable for a gentleman of his standing.

Taking the Flying Scotsman from London, where he and his wife had spent a few days with their son, to York was one thing. From thereon in they were consigned to travelling along branch lines whose trains were quite provincial and whose frequent changes were nothing short of criminal. York to Malton and then change at Malton for the Redcar train, disembark at Shearing's Vale where his man was to pick him up and drive him to Beechings, his country pile, hopefully in good time for dinner.

A Strange Encounter at Little Hubery

His wife, Lady Agnes, was a placid, good-natured woman who, far from hating train journeys, secretly enjoyed them and looked forward to travelling by Flying Scotsman with all the relish of a school boy on his first trip aboard a locomotive. When it came to travelling on the branch lines however, she was in full agreement with her husband, as the trains were often late and run-down, with hard horse-hair seating and dirty windows. The train to Shearing's Vale was particularly unpleasant, a two coach, non-corridor, snorting beast of a train, quite often crowded and always cold and poorly maintained. Unfortunately, it was either this or a direct train from York to Redcar and having to return at Redcar on the same grotty little train all the way back to Shearing's Vale. She was hoping however, as they would be returning quite late to the Vale, that the train would be less packed.

She looked across at her husband and smiled to herself. He was a dreadful snob, and she often wondered what people thought of him. He was a proud man and had been one of the country's top barristers. But he had been slowing down recently and his hands were gnarled and crippled by arthritis. His temper hadn't been curbed any though. Pompous old fool, she thought, smiling fondly. Sir Gregory looked up from his newspaper and wondered what was amusing his wife so.

Chapter Four

Miss Ellen Potter had been offered a position as head of English and literature studies at a boarding school for girls in Northumberland and was taking the journey mid-term to begin her new post, as her predecessor had been taken ill. Instead of taking the train direct from York where she lived with her sister, she was to take the train to Malton and change there for Redcar, where she would call in on an elderly relative who'd not been too good recently.

She didn't mind the detour. She thought a trip across the wild Yorkshire moorland would be exciting. Maybe she would see the gloomy, austere form of Wuthering Heights from her carriage window, or the burnt-out shell of the Rochester house up on the hill. Maybe she'd meet her Heathcliffe on the train, a dark and brooding stranger who would catch her eye and whisk her off to a life as lady of the manor. At twenty-eight, Ellen's head was still as full of romantic notions as it had been at eighteen, although for a lady in her position as department head at the school, she really should have known better.

She was lucky to have been offered such a good position, but the school had been in dire need of a replacement teacher and that, along with her exemplary reference from her last employer and the fact that her elderly aunt in Redcar had been headmistress there, had stood her in good stead with the school. She knew her sister and her aunt had conspired to get her out of York as quickly as possible and understandably. For reasons known only to herself, she blushed a deep shade of crimson, quickly burying her head in her bag under the pretence of fishing for a handkerchief so no-one could witness her indignity.

It had been a messy affair truly, but not one entirely of her making. She thought of George and brushed away a tear before composing herself and powdering her nose, quickly snapping shut her compact mirror after receiving a look of distain from a passing elderly lady.

A Strange Encounter at Little Hubery

She longed for a cigarette but disapproved of ladies smoking in public. Although Ellen was learned and extremely attractive, she was nearing spinster age, a fact not entirely lost on her, although she exhibited all the naivety and vulnerability in public of a woman half her age. She felt extremely uncomfortable under the glare of older ladies and was in truth far more at ease in the company of children. She looked forward to the safe and comfortable confines of the school where she might begin writing her long-planned novel. She knew she would have a good life at the school, although she'd not entirely given up on meeting her Mr Darcy yet.

She thought she might treat herself to a new book from Smiths, the newsagent. A Bronte classic perhaps, or maybe even the new Agatha Christie novel if she could get hold of it. Who better than the mistress of suspense when you're watching a desolate, storm-tossed moor from an empty train carriage window, the silent landscape lit only by flashes of lightning, the occasional tree, twisted and gnarled, casting eerie shadows on the ground? Ellen was much affected by atmospherics, and as she looked through the refreshment room window at the gathering clouds, a sudden shiver of excitement ran up and down her spine. She was looking forward to starting her new life at the school, and she could feel that something was building up, could almost sense it impending.

As she turned to leave the room, such a strange, almost cruel smile veiled her features that anyone witnessing it from outside on the platform would be left to wonder at what unpleasant thoughts could darken so lovely and gentle a face.

Chapter Five

Professor Victor Rose was weary. He'd had a long journey and he still had to make a couple of changes and travel another fifty mile or so before he was home. He had been visiting his friend, Professor Sidney Miles, a dean of faculty at Kings College Cambridge, where he'd enjoyed first class hospitality, a fine single malt and setting the world to rights with his friend, as well as intellectual discourse with his former colleagues and students.

Professor Rose enjoyed his bi-annual visits to his beloved Cambridge, but they really tired him out and he was looking forward to seeing hearth and home again. He lived in a cosy cottage by the sea in Saltburn, with his dog Scout and his house-keeper Mrs Carr, and apart from the aforementioned, he rarely saw another soul. His was a quiet, peaceful and quite unremarkable life, and he liked it that way. A self-confirmed bachelor, he had dedicated his life to the pursuit of learning. His small library, his coastal walks and Mrs Carr's fine cooking were all he needed to live a full and contented life.

His train arrived at Doncaster where a few got off and even fewer got on. A family of four with two very excited boys joined him in his carriage and seemed bound for their holidays in Edinburgh. Their father was teasing them about joining a haggis hunt when they got to Scotland, and the little boys' eyes shone with anticipation. The professor couldn't suppress a smile as one of the boys asked if the hunt would be on horseback and the boys' mother clicked her tongue in feigned annoyance at her husband's teasing. They soon settled in and gave up their tickets to the inspector and Victor relaxed back into his seat and closed his eyes for a moment.

'Mustn't sleep,' he mumbled to himself, fearing he would lose his connection. He would soon be in York where he planned to have a nice cup of tea and a pastry before catching the train to Malton.

Chapter Six

Lance Corporal Robert Newton, of the newly amalgamated 4th/7th Royal Dragoon Guards, pulled the collar of his greatcoat tight around his neck against the biting wind that seemed to whip up from nowhere. He lit a cigarette, shielding the flame from the wind, and wandered up and down the empty platform. He had never seen Malton so quiet. Harrogate in contrast had been a hive of activity, and he was secretly glad to be away from the crowds. Peace and quiet was just what he needed now, time to think

He'd been in India for the past six months and was now to be stationed at Catterick Camp. He was currently on leave and had been visiting his mother in Harrogate before going to meet his wife and daughter in Redcar. He sat down on the bench and ran his hand across his face. He wasn't at all looking forward to the inquiry he would face when his leave was over. Talk about wrong place, wrong time! Damn him, that fellow had deserved everything he got, no-one could deny that. He hadn't been involved directly but he hadn't exactly been forthcoming either, as a keeper of the peace or as a witness.

He wrung his hands and a shadow fell across his troubled face when he thought of what had passed and what was to follow as a consequence. He knew he was early and had a long wait for his train, but everything seemed long drawn out and tiresome to him since that day three weeks ago. Truth was nobody knew he'd witnessed the event. He realised people could place him close to the scene, but nobody could prove he'd actually watched the action unfold from where he was positioned. Should he lie to save himself and his colleagues and friends, or tell the truth and face the consequences?

A sudden streak of lightning, unannounced by any rumble of thunder, lit up the platform like a flare, and Lance Corporal Robert Newton buried his head deeper into his greatcoat.

On the opposite platform, from the window of a shadowy waiting room, a silent figure watched.

Chapter Seven

Percy shovelled the remaining pieces of coal onto the waiting room fire before refilling the scuttle from the coal store behind the station buildings. He'd be thinking of lighting the gas lamps soon. It was getting dark early now and the bloody storm clouds didn't help any. He could have sworn he heard thunder a couple of minutes ago. Thunder! In autumn! Not unheard of certainly, but definitely odd.

He couldn't shake off the unsettled feeling he'd had all day. He didn't like storms at the best of times, not since he was about seven and he'd seen his friend struck by lightning as they played on the moor. This one was set to be a right humdinger. There'd be trouble on the line for certain if the storm broke, especially with the wind getting up.

He could hear the wireless from Arthur's office and he knew the world service had just announced a severe weather warning for all coastal stations. Arthur was much affected by the weather and he was certainly in a strange mood today. *I'll take him a cup of tea in a minute or two,* Percy thought. *That ought to cheer him up a bit.*

A sudden pelt of rain on the windows made him look up, and the young couple who'd just left the waiting room came running in breathless and laughing, equally surprised by the suddenness of the downpour.

'We're in for one tonight,' the young man commented to Percy. 'Better batten down the hatches. That wind's getting up something fierce. I hope there are no cancellations to trains. We've a distance to go yet.'

'Well, we've heard nothing so far sir,' Percy replied. 'But I'll certainly keep you posted if we do.'

Chapter Eight

Professor Rose was sure he'd seen the gentleman who'd just entered the refreshment room somewhere before.

'Oh dear,' said Lady Agnes, 'it's rather full, isn't it?' The professor stood and motioned the couple over.

'You're more than welcome to join me at my table,' he offered with a smile. 'I'm afraid you'll never find a quiet time to visit York station.'

'Awful journey home,' Sir Gregory said, after introducing himself and his wife. 'And now the weather's turned.'

'And set to get worse I'm afraid,' said Professor Rose, smiling at Lady Agnes. 'Have you far to go?' The conversation was interrupted by two young lads who tore into the refreshment room, chased each other around the tables and then fled when an angry-looking man came out from behind the counter.'

'Young hooligans. Should be publicly flogged,' bellowed Sir Gregory, and one or two turned in their seats to look at him. Lady Agnes smiled sheepishly at the professor, whose newly arrived pastry had suddenly demanded his utmost attention.

Ellen noticed the young soldier sitting on the platform at Malton and thought him rather handsome. She paraded past him to the bench further down and took out her new Agatha Christie novel, *Murder in Mesopotamia*. He glanced briefly, appreciating the female form, but it was clear his mind was elsewhere. She half wished she'd gone back to the waiting room as it was starting to rain, but the train was due soon and the waiting room was down the far end of the platform, so she decided to stay put.

She thought how quiet the station was for the time of day. Apart from herself and the soldier it seemed only a handful or so, including the two elderly gentlemen and the rather well-dressed lady, were waiting for the train to Redcar. She didn't mind that at all. It meant she could read

A Strange Encounter at Little Hubery

in peace and daydream to her heart's content. In fact she hoped to have a compartment to herself.

Soon the two coach non-corridor train pulled alongside the platform and its passengers jumped aboard eagerly, happy to continue their respective journeys out of the biting wind. Ellen looked through the window of one compartment and was startled by the face that stared back at her. It was a face she knew, whose dark, hate-filled eyes glared at her with pure malice. Her heart began to pound and she felt a trickle of perspiration run down her back. For what seemed like an age she was unable to pull away. She stood rooted to the spot until a hand grabbed the carriage door and a couple pushed their way into the compartment.

'But it couldn't be,' she told herself. 'It's impossible.' She walked quickly down to the next coach and saw the three distinguished elders and the soldier climbing into the second and third compartments. She hastily jumped into the first, her heart beating wildly, fear shrouding her like a widow's cape.

'Impossible,' she repeated, closing her eyes and breathing deeply, trying to regain composure. She was joined seconds before departure by an older lady who smiled at her sweetly before settling down with her book. Ellen smiled back, glad of the company.

As the train pulled out of the station she could see two or three people milling about on the platform. An angry-looking man was bending the ear of a poor porter, and a beautiful young girl caught her eye before quickly looking away. Ellen thought how sad and lost the girl had looked and found herself wondering about her fellow travellers and where their journeys would lead them.

Soon her attention was drawn to the craggy moorland beyond the rain-lashed window. The occasional lonely dwelling, with its cosy lamp-lit window, looked to Ellen like a beacon on a storm-tossed sea and made her feel alone and displaced. The wind howled across the open moor, hammering the train. When the lightning flashed, bathing the wilderness beyond in an eerie glow, she imagined she could see all manner of unearthly creatures lurking in the bushes and waiting in the shadows to engulf them in the event of the train stopping and their being stranded out there on the wild moor.

A Strange Encounter at Little Hubery

She picked up her book and wished she had bought something a little more light-hearted.

'Soon be home dear,' smiled the old lady kindly, sensing her growing unease. Ellen thought of her aunt's fire-lit parlour and a good hot supper and settled back into her seat and rested her eyes.

'Of course,' said the professor, smiling. 'I thought I recognised you in the refreshment room at York. You were the judge in that kidnapping case, with the little boy. Dreadful business that. The fellow hanged I believe?'

'He did,' said Sir Gregory. 'But hanging was too good for him after what he did to that poor boy. Given the choice, I'd have had him on the rack. A prolonged and painful death is all a scoundrel like that deserves.' The professor winced and Lady Agnes smiled apologetically.

'Come now, Gregory. Justice has been served and the man has paid the ultimate price for his crime. Let God be his judge now.'

'Hmm!' grumbled Sir Gregory 'And may he be condemned to burn in hellfire forever more!

Now, let that be an end to it. Where's my newspaper?'

Professor Rose smiled as Lady Agnes raised her eyes to heaven in exasperation. Soon enough the compartment was still as the journey progressed and the two gentlemen settled down to their papers, only the occasional grumble from Sir Gregory about the hard unyielding seats or his nagging arthritis breaking the silence as they steamed across the darkening windswept moor.

Alone in his compartment, Robert was feeling increasingly agitated. He lit another cigarette and noticed the slight trembling of his hand. It wasn't the storm that bothered him, nor was he particularly worried about the inquiry to come, for he'd already decided that he would feign ignorance of any knowledge of the incident. He was only being called as a potential witness after all. It was the only option if he was to carry on with his military career. His own survival and that of his family depended on it.

Given the option of turning back time, he would certainly have intervened. Stopped his

A Strange Encounter at Little Hubery

comrades short of taking the man's life however much he deplored him for what he was and the abominations he had committed. But there was nothing he could do now. The man was dead! Ruining the lives and careers of three good men wouldn't bring him back. His decision was made.

Even with the weight of the decision off his shoulders, Robert still felt uneasy. It was a creepy sensation, almost like a feeling of impending doom. His stomach was tense and knotted and his throat was dry. He looked out at the moor just as a flash of lightning illuminated the backdrop. Through the sparkle of raindrops on the grimy window, he saw this particular part of the moorland was thick with shrub, and he imagined as he stared into the wilderness a thousand pairs of eyes watching him from deep within the shadowy leaves and prickly hedgerows. A sudden feeling of panic overcame the soldier and he turned away from the window. Pushing himself into the corner, he rested his head against the wall and closed his eyes until the feeling subsided.

Chapter Nine

The station at Little Hubery had been quiet since the departure of the runaway couple on the two-forty-five to Redcar. Percy knew they were taking the scenic route to Gretna. They weren't the first nor would they be the last and he wished them well. He thought of his own wife and felt a pain akin to mourning. His marriage was in trouble, he could not deny. He loved his wife more than life itself but his uncontrollable fits of jealousy were ruining everything. Since she'd taken up painting classes at the church hall, his imagination had run riot and with no evidence or provocation at all. What the hell was wrong with him? Why couldn't he just enjoy being loved?

He heard Arthur through the door singing along to Guy Lombardo's 'You're Driving Me Crazy.'

A Strange Encounter at Little Hubery

'You've got that about right my friend,' he thought grimly. Maybe Arthur had the right idea living the uncomplicated bachelor life.

All at once, he was overcome by the feeling of no longer being alone. The thunder roared above and the lightning came in flashes. The rain, carried by gale force winds, beat against the windows with vigour. The fire burned brightly enough in the grate, but the waiting room seemed to have gotten darker. Colder too! He shivered as he lit the gas lamps. He should have done it an hour ago really. This bloody station was creepy enough at the best of times without this awful storm, he thought, rubbing his arms to keep warm.

All of a sudden he felt certain he was being watched and that whoever it was, was right behind him. He'd not heard the waiting room door go and Arthur was still in his office singing. He turned slowly and gasped when he saw the man standing there. He was tall, much taller then Percy who was by no means a small man, but painfully thin. His hair, his skin, even his suit, which was bone-dry although he carried no coat, were waxy and grey and his eyes, which were also a colourless grey, were devoid and empty. Percy couldn't suppress a shudder when the man suddenly grinned at him, a humourless sinister grin that never quite reached his eyes.

'Single, first to Redcar please.' His voice was monotonous and low, and Percy could barely make out his words over the sudden clap of thunder that seemed so much closer than the last.

But where had he come from? Percy was sure he hadn't entered by the platform. The only other way was through the booking office and he'd been in there the whole time.

'The next Redcar train will terminate here sir, due to signalling problems at Clarings Brook. I'm not sure when the next through train will be Sir, on accounts of the weather.

The man carried on grinning

'Never mind,' he said. 'I'm quite happy waiting here.' Another streak of lightning and his face was bathed in an eerie glow, highlighting the waxen pallor of his skin, the shadows accentuating the sunken hollows of his eyes.

A Strange Encounter at Little Hubery

Pull yourself together man, Percy thought, turning his head away. The poor man's obviously ill.

Percy waited until the man had seated himself beside the fire, noticing how even the glow of the flames failed to add warmth to his dead skin. He wondered as to how a man could walk across a wooden floor and sit on a creaky wooden chair without making a sound. Everything about him was odd. As he pulled out a newspaper from his briefcase and began to read, he still wore the sinister grin that had unnerved Percy so on first meeting him. He was still staring at the man when Arthur walked through from his office.

'Does the gentleman know that the next train terminates here, Percy?' Percy jumped. He hadn't heard Arthur come in.

'Percy?'

'Erm yes, yes I told him. He said he's happy to wait.' Arthur sighed and approached the passenger.

'Good afternoon sir,' said Arthur. 'I'm sorry for your wait. It is just a minor signal problem and we hope to have it fixed soon.' The man smiled warmly at the stationmaster.

'No problem at all, I'm in no hurry and quite content sitting here.'

A Stranger's Tale

He knew he'd never be able to keep her in the style she'd been accustomed to. The Mayor's daughter, how could he? Him, a simple bank clerk. What did he have to offer a lady like that really? Everyone was surprised when they became a couple and even more so when she accepted his proposal. But he knew she genuinely loved him as he did her, with all his heart.

He'd heard a rumour that Mr Sykes, the assistant bank manager, was to retire, and if he did that meant that Norman would be next in line for his job, leaving a supervisory position vacant. Surely it was his turn to move up the ranks? God knows he'd been there long enough. How proud of him Betty would be then, and it meant more money. He could buy her that ring she wanted from the jewellers in the high street. He was doing well at the bank. No-one could deny that. Why only that morning he'd taken in four new accounts. Lucrative ones, too. Fat landlords looking for somewhere to deposit their tenants' weekly payments into. Hundreds of pounds they had in their accounts. He'd looked on enviously as they made their deposits, thinking how a few shillings of that a week into his own account would make a world of difference. Just a shilling or two, always from different accounts. Nobody would miss it…would they?

Chapter Ten

Little Hubery Station stood, bleached by lightning, its rough stonework standing out against the darkening backdrop of the moor. Through the tall windows, the flickering of the gas lamps and the amber glow of the fire made the station seem cosy and welcoming to the disheartened passengers who disembarked from the terminated Redcar train. A man in a military coat, a young lady, two elderly gents and a well-dressed lady were the only passengers left on the train when it terminated at Little Hubery due to a signal failure in the next section of the line. Although clearly upset at having their journey disrupted, only one of the older gentlemen made a fuss.

The engine standing at the platform uncoupled to make its way back to Malton. The passengers joined the other one already in the waiting room, but he seemed not to notice their arrival, never once looking up from his newspaper as they crowded around the fire.

'It appears we may be here for some time,' said the professor. 'Have you been here long sir?' he asked the man already seated.

'Hardly any time at all,' the man replied.

'Would you like me to stay on Arthur? Looks like you'll be here for quite a while.' Percy looked in on Arthur when his shift finished at five-thirty. He would often walk home from the station to his cottage on the other side of Little Hubery, but when the weather turned he would catch a lift home with Walter, the station porter.

'I'll be fine Percy,' said Arthur, looking up from his paperwork. 'I'll put a call through to Clarings Brook and then I'll speak to the passengers. How are they?' He nodded towards the waiting room where the displaced passengers where gathered

'Couple of them a bit restless,' Percy replied, 'and there's an old fella looks bound to kick up a stink if he's kept waiting, but mostly fine. Arthur...' Percy paused hesitantly. 'Did you

A Strange Encounter at Little Hubery

notice anything odd about that man who was here before the others came off the train?'

'Not at all,' said Arthur throwing down his pen. 'Why do you ask?'

Percy shrugged his shoulders.

'Ah, nothing much.' He grinned. 'Just seemed a bit, well, queer is all. Anyway I'll be off then if there's nothing else I can do?'

'No more trains tonight, folks,' said Arthur, coming in from his office. 'I'm really sorry'

A collective moan could be heard from the passengers in the waiting room. It hung in the air like a mist.

'What's the meaning of this?' stormed the elderly gentleman. 'My man is waiting with the car at Shearing's Vale.'

'I'm sorry, sir?'

'Name's Barnes, Sir Gregory Barnes,' he huffed. 'I demand to know—'

'If you would please sit down, sir. There's a fallen tree on the line at Shearing's Vale, probably the result of the high winds we've been having. I'm afraid no-one's going anywhere from this station tonight.'

'Please, sir, I-I have to be somewhere.' The girl who had been sat in a shadowy corner, previously unseen by the stationmaster, stepped forward. She clutched tightly at her suitcase and coloured when she spoke.

'I'm sorry, Miss,' said Arthur. 'There's an inn at Little Hubery with rooms. But that's over a mile and half away across moorland and in this weather I—'

'Oh,' the girl said quietly and melted back into the shadows.'

'But surely man, there's some mode of transport to get us to Hubery? Perhaps from there we can go on to Shearing's Vale, or my man could pick me up from the inn?' said Sir Gregory, his face red with exasperation.

'I'm afraid I have no car, sir, and anyhow you'll find no trackless leaving Hubery tonight. It would seem as though there's no traffic getting through or your gentleman could pick you up from here. I can call Shearing's Vale and speak with him if you like, sir. It may be prudent for you to send him home.' As though giving credence to the stationmaster's statement, the wind suddenly howled in protest and drove the rain hard against the windows.

A Strange Encounter at Little Hubery

'But that's absurd...'

'I suggest we let the man speak.' The soldier stepped forward. Sir Gregory turned to him angrily, ready to answer back, but something in the soldier's manner made him think again.

'Thank you, sir,' the stationmaster continued. 'I am unable to leave my post but perhaps a couple of the gentlemen would like to walk into town? You sir,' he said to the man who had walked into the station. 'You came here on foot I believe. Are you local? Perhaps you could send someone back with a car?'

The man looked up from his paper for the first time. A strange smile played about his lips and his eyes shone in the glow of the fire. It seemed as though he was enjoying the excitement.

'I'm not local, no sir,' he replied. 'But I know well the unpredictability and the wildness of the moor and I think I'd rather stay here, sir, if no-one minds.'

'Really!' said Sir Gregory incredulously. 'What kind of fellow are you?' The man merely smiled and carried on reading. Sir Gregory was furious.

'I'll go!' said Professor Rose. 'Perhaps...' he said, nodding to the soldier, 'if this young man will come with me?'

'You can't go, professor,' protested Lady Agnes. She looked at the stationmaster pleadingly. 'Is there no-one else at the station sir?'

The soldier came forward.

'I'll go alone,' he said. 'I'll send back a car.' Pulling on his greatcoat, he made for the door.

'Be careful, sir, please!' Arthur called out over the howling wind. 'The moor is dangerous. Please don't stray from the path—'

The door slammed and his sentence was cut off.

'I hope he will be safe,' said Lady Agnes anxiously.'

'I'm sure he will,' said Sir Gregory. 'Fellow had a local accent. I'm sure he's no stranger to the moor.'

The stationmaster looked at him coldly.

'We may have to stay here for the next few hours, until the storm dies down or the roads are cleared. Wireless says we're in for an almighty storm, but we've plenty of coal for the fire and

A Strange Encounter at Little Hubery

I've tea and Horlicks in my office, if you're not afraid to drink from mugs.'

'Dear God,' said Sir Gregory, sitting back down and rubbing his arthritic knees.

'I'll fetch some more coal and get a good blaze going. I suggest you try making yourselves comfortable, at least for now.'

The girl stood up.

'I'll help you,' she said. The stationmaster thanked her and the two left the subdued silence of the waiting room.

Chapter Eleven

Robert stepped out onto the platform, the biting wind stinging the exposed flesh of his face and lashing him with rain. Lightning illuminated the platform for a second or two and he was certain he saw a fleeting shadow down by the lavatories. Maybe there was someone else at the station after all.

'Hello!' he called out, but the wind must have carried his voice because the figure disappeared towards the end of the platform. Am I seeing things? Robert thought. It was now pitch black; the gas lanterns were giving out little light and casting eerie shadows along the platform.

'Hello!' Robert felt certain the man had heard him, because he turned and the soldier saw a pale face illuminated by the moonlight during a brief break in the clouds. Robert waved and the figure seemed to freeze for a moment.

A Strange Encounter at Little Hubery

'Hello there, sir. Can you help us?' Robert called out again, but the figure turned and ran down onto the tracks and out of sight.

When Robert stepped out of the shelter of the station buildings and onto the quiet side road, he felt the full force of the storm

'Arrgh!' he called out, shielding his face as he staggered backwards. Thunder roared overhead and the landscape was suddenly lit up before him. He could see the road ahead, the only road into town across open moorland. If he accidentally wandered from the path, he could easily be lost on the moor. As a solider he was well used to trekking across rough terrain, but the moor was fully exposed to the elements and the ground would be sodden and hard to tackle. What if he came across an area of marshland? They were so close to the sea, he could easily walk into a bog. No-one would hear his cries on a stormy night like this. No-one would be there to help him.

Tentatively he made his way toward the open moor. To the left-hand side of the road was a thick hedge. This would help him at least part of the way. While ever he felt the rough hedge at his shoulder, he knew he was sticking to the path. He tripped and almost fell on the uneven surface of the verge and cursed when he remembered that he had come out without a torch. His mind was clearly elsewhere. Only a fool would attempt to do what he was doing in total darkness. Overhead the moon was now totally obscured by the clouds that rolled like angry waves on a storm-tossed sea. He was already soaked through, and he could feel the rain running down the back of his collar and penetrating the soft leather of his boots. His skin felt tight against the vicious wind, and he could barely see ahead of him. What dangers did he face from vehicles out on an open road on a night like this? Once more he cursed his stupidity and wished more than anything he hadn't left the warmth of the waiting room hearth.

Chapter Twelve

Four people regarded each another in morose silence. The waiting room was full of ethereal shapes cast by the dimly lit gaslights, but a good fire blazed in the grate and the shadows, bathed in the amber glow, danced wretchedly across the walls and ceiling. A clock ticked sonorously above the mantelpiece, but even that was silenced by the deafening roar of the wind that sped along the hollow, hitting the exposed station building with full force and rattling the ill-fitting windows in their frames.

'I hope that young man will be safe out there on the moor,' began Lady Agnes.

'Fellow's trained for that kind of thing,' replied her husband gruffly. 'So long as he returns or sends a car soon, we should be just fine. I should hate to miss a good dinner.' The professor gave the man a good hard stare and from his place by the fire, the stranger grinned and shook his head.

'Are you going far Mr...?' The professor turned to look at the man who had so far remained silent.

'Travers,' said the man, smiling. 'And it would appear not.' He dropped his head, signifying that he had no wish for further conversation. Lady Agnes looked over and was about to introduce herself and her husband when the booking office door opened and the stationmaster and the girl returned with the drinks.

'Make way for the cup that cheers.' The stationmaster smiled, and despite grumblings from the judge about the state of the mugs, they were all grateful for the hot drinks. Travers, being closest, got up a decent blaze. Then Arthur went next door and brought in the wireless, and amid the Al Bowelly's and Artie Shaw's, they listened out for the news and weather reports.

Suddenly and inexplicably, the lights in the waiting room dimmed. The flames from the lamps flickered and spluttered as though a draught had crept in from somewhere and was

A Strange Encounter at Little Hubery

threatening to blow them clean out. Even the light from the fire was subdued. The flames cowered behind large chunks of coal and the clock above the mantle became unnervingly loud.

The howling of the wind out on the moor now sounded more like the cries of animals in distress, an eerie, wailing sound. The ladies looked at each other, wide-eyed and nervous. Even the men huddled a little closer to the hearth.

'Don't worry folks.' The stationmaster smiled reassuringly at Ellen and Lady Agnes. 'The station has withstood more severe weather than this and is still standing to tell the tale. Pity the poor signalmen isolated in their boxes or the gangers out trying to clear the line. There's always folks worse off than yourself.'

Lady Agnes smiled back at the man with his kind twinkling eyes and his infectious optimism and was about to agree when a strange, high-pitched whistling sound silenced all. The wireless, in the middle of playing Cab Calloway, suddenly cut off and all was silent. For a moment or two only static could be heard, and then it seemed as though someone was retuning. There were snatches of what sounded like foreign radio stations before the announcement of an urgent broadcast. All turned expectantly towards the instrument, but the voice that emanated from it wasn't that of the broadcaster. It was slow, dragged out and deep as if it being wound down, so much so that the words were hard to decipher. All the passengers could make out was

'…all judgements will be passed…' and '…before this night ends.'

'Oh dear!' said Lady Agnes, and Ellen remembered the face on the train and shuddered.

'What's the meaning of this, sir?' said the barrister, turning to face the stationmaster. 'Is this meant to be some kind of joke? Because if it is I—'

Suddenly from a dark corner behind Ellen came a low chuckle, evil and sinister. The girl screamed and jumped up, moving close to Lady Agnes, who put a maternal arm around her shoulder.

'Who's there?' bellowed Sir Gregory. 'Come out man and make yourself known.'

Arthur rushed to the back of the waiting room but there was no-one there. He turned to

A Strange Encounter at Little Hubery

face the others in bewilderment. All at once the wind got up and the flames raced up the chimney to meet it. An overhead clap of thunder was so loud that it had the ladies wincing. The stationmaster stood dumbstruck in the far corner, and the wireless returned to 'Minnie the Moocher' as if nothing had happened.

A sudden but brief flash of lightning illuminated the scene, highlighting the professor's strange expression. He was staring into the shadows of the chimneybreast at Travers, who stared back, his eyes shining with excitement and a strange and sinister smile about his lips…

Chapter Thirteen

Robert's eyes had become accustomed to the dark, but his vision was still impeded by the wind and rain which seemed much worse out here on the exposed moor. He had left the security of the hedge behind a good way back, and only the firmness of the road underfoot guided him along his way. He needed to be careful not to go wandering into the middle of the road, in the path of any approaching vehicles, but the further into his journey he got, the least likely it seemed that anyone would be out there on the moor in this foul weather.

Why was he here anyway? Why was he wandering the stricken moor alone on a night like this? He didn't mind being holed up in the station for a couple of hours. Certainly his wife would worry a little if he were late, but he was sure the stationmaster would allow him to call her. Anyway, that didn't warrant him risking

A Strange Encounter at Little Hubery

life and limb so that pompous old bastard back at the station would be home in time for dinner.

He turned and tried to gage the distance between himself and the station. He seemed to have been out there for ages, but in truth he couldn't have come more than a quarter of a mile.

He was suddenly aware of another presence, and with all the sharpened senses and awareness of a soldier who had seen action, he knew that he was being watched. The moorland lit up again briefly, and he scanned the landscape looking for signs of a predator. The land lay flat and treeless around him. There was nowhere to hide. All the same he somehow knew he was being hunted, that unseen eyes watched him from out on the desolate moor. He felt exposed and vulnerable and turned this way and that, not knowing whether to turn back or move on, unsure in which direction the danger lay but knowing that someone or something lay in wait for him in the darkness.

The wind screamed like a banshee and he felt disorientated, lost for a moment. The lightning flashed, and he saw shadows moving out there on the wild, inhospitable moorland. Then all at once, the wind died down and he stood there alone in the pouring rain. All was silent, then he heard a cry, a scream of terror and pain that almost stopped his heart. Was someone lost? Trapped and in peril?

'Hello,' he cried out, cupping his hands together to help the sound to carry. 'Hello, is anyone out there?' Again the scream rang out across the desolate moor. Someone was afraid and in terrible pain. Robert ran around blindly trying to detect the source of the sound, which seemed to come from everywhere at once. Only when he found his feet sinking into the sodden ground did he turn and retrace his steps. He stood on the hard standing shaking with the cold and fear, when as suddenly as they had begun, the screams stopped.

'Hello,' he shouted. 'Please tell me where you are, then I can help you.'

All at once he was overcome by a terror the likes of which he had never known before, and he knew beyond a shadow of doubt that there was no-one in danger out there on the moor. That the whole thing was a trap, to lure him from the safety of the path to his death. He turned to run but fear held him tight in its grip,

A Strange Encounter at Little Hubery

and he felt a hot breath on the back of his neck and heard a voice that made his blood run cold.

'Robert!' the voice whispered in his ear. *'Robert, help me!'*

'No!' screamed Robert, his hands reaching out to cover his ears. 'You're not real! You can't be real, you're dead. I know you're dead!'

Still the whispering continued, low and breathy, as though it was inside his own head.

'Help me!' the voice implored. Robert closed his eyes tightly and when he opened them, he looked straight into the eyes of his dead comrade. The flat, dead, vacant eyes of a man he had watched die.

'You could have saved me, Lance Corporal,' said the shade mournfully. Robert was suddenly overcome by such feelings of evil and loathing that he turned on his heel and ran. The wind whipped up into a frenzy and the rain was torrential. An overhead clap of thunder boomed like an explosion directly above him, and he whimpered as he ran blindly into the storm.

From all around him the moor was alive with screeching and howling, and somewhere deep in the back of his mind an evil sniggering voice taunted him as he ran.

Jack C. Phillips

'You could have helped me, Robert...'

Chapter Fourteen

Robert burst into the waiting room as if the devil himself were chasing him, and seeing the expression on his face, his fellow travellers wouldn't be wrong in supposing he was.

Everyone jumped as he fell through the door and on to his knees, soaked and panting after his ordeal. The professor was the first to run over to him and helped him to his feet.

'S-sorry folks,' Robert managed to stammer breathlessly. 'I co— I couldn't get halfway across the moor without the storm d-driving me back.'

'Well that's that then,' said Sir Gregory and slumped down as though wearily resigned to his fate. He took out his pipe. 'Nothing more a fellow can do.'

The ladies fussed over Robert, pulling him up a chair by the fire and removing his wet coat and boots. Arthur came back in with towels and a steaming mug of tea, which the soldier accepted gratefully.

'Any more news?' he said, nodding at the wireless.

The people in the waiting room looked at each other nervously.

'We're in for one hell of a night my friend,' said Travers from the chimney corner.

'Hmm!' said Sir Gregory through his pipe and nothing more.

'Let's make the best of a bad situation then,' said the professor, standing to poke the fire.

'It's an intolerable situation,' grunted Sir Gregory. 'My wife and I are quite unused to…'

Lady Agnes walked back to her seat from where she'd been tending to the soldier, whose teeth had not stopped chattering.

'Be quiet Gregory dear! I haven't had this much excitement in my life since the King's funeral.' Gregory looked up at his wife in shock, and Ellen grinned at Robert. It was obvious the woman had never stood up to her domineering husband before.

'I could check and see if the way's clear up to the house. I'm sure the ladies would be more comfortable there,' cut in Arthur. 'But that

A Strange Encounter at Little Hubery

stream's fast flowing at the best of times and if it's swollen, it could easily have taken that rickety old bridge with it.'

Sir Gregory was about to reply, but a stern look from his wife silenced him.

'That's very kind of you Mr...?' Lady Agnes smiled warmly at the stationmaster.

'Please, call me Arthur.'

Arthur shivered as he stepped out onto the platform. This certainly is a freak storm, he thought to himself. A storm of this ferocity would normally blow itself out within a matter of hours. This had been building up all day and seemed set to rage all night. The wind and rain beat at his face and head, and he rubbed his eyes to clear his vision.

He didn't fancy taking the bridge so he crossed the lines, knowing that he wasn't in any danger from oncoming trains. Even being in his own territory, he felt vulnerable and exposed, and he could easily imagine the soldier feeling disoriented and lost out there on the open moor.

Over on the down platform he thought he saw movement from the corner of his eye, by the goods sheds.

'Pull yourself together man,' he said, trying hard to suppress a shudder. 'The storm's playing tricks with your mind is all.'

When he reached the sheds, he decided to take a quick look around to satisfy his curiosity and check that all was well. Above the wailing of the storm, he could hear the creaking and groaning of the sheds as the padlocked doors strained against the pull. There was no lighting at the back except for inside the sheds themselves, and the hulking black silhouettes of the buildings stood proud against the stormy wind-tossed clouds, behind which the lightening flickered and the moon snatched occasional glimpses through the breaks.

'Bloody hell,' said Arthur, flicking on his torch and taking a quick look around. He wished the passengers had not been stranded at his station. He longed for home. A bit of supper and a stiff brandy by the fire with his dog and his wireless before bed would be just what the doctor ordered. Instead he was stuck at the

A Strange Encounter at Little Hubery

station listening to that bloody KC and his constant moaning.

He'd recognised the whining old sod from the newspaper. Hadn't he recently received an accolade for sending that kidnapper to the gallows? He shuddered. Horrible business. For what that bastard had done to that little boy, he deserved to swing. Barnes was right about that.

He stepped out from the shelter of the sheds and an almighty gust of wind threatened to blow him clean off his feet.

'Bloody hell,' he repeated, his hand shaking as he held onto his torch.

He walked up the narrow path that led to the bridge and home and groaned with dismay at the sight that greeted him. The bridge and most of the bank had been washed away, and the water level was still rising.

'Oh no,' he groaned. 'No, no!' He thought he could hear his dog howling in the house, but it could only have been the wind. He walked closer to the river and he could see the debris of the old bridge and other detritus had become wedged between the two banks and were forming a dam, the water building up on one side at an alarming level. There was no danger to his home, but if it carried on swelling at this level, there may well be some damage to the sheds and their equipment.

He looked around in desperation. Should he go back to the waiting room and ask the soldier and that man Travers to help him clear the debris? No, he couldn't risk placing passengers in harm's way, and he knew there would be no-one else around who could help him with the signalman unable to leave his box.

'Think man, think!' he scolded himself. 'Old Albert would've known what to do.'

At the thought of his father, he was filled with feelings of guilt and remorse. He quickly cleared his head and tried to think. Nearby he spotted an old wooden prop with a hooked end. He knew the gangers sometimes used them to clear debris from the track. If only I can knock the top clear, he thought, the water could flow freely again.

Taking the prop in his free hand, he walked carefully toward the water's edge. Once or twice he almost slipped in the mud, quickly regaining his balance by leaning on the prop.

He squatted, feet apart on the bank close to the dam, and once he was sure of his balance, he

A Strange Encounter at Little Hubery

took the flat end of the prop and began poking at the loser debris at the top. One or two small planks from the footbridge came loose, and he guided them towards the bank at his feet and plucked them out, kneeling on one but careful not to lean too far over.

He tried again, but the dam was tightly wedged and wouldn't budge, so he turned the prop around and taking the hooked side, he wrapped it around a protruding branch half way down the dam wall.

'If only I can get some good leverage on this, I might get the whole thing to topple,' he thought aloud. He pulled firmly, but the branch wouldn't budge. Keeping one hand on the ground for balance, he pulled a little harder and the branch moved a fraction. He tried to unhook the prop to grab the wood a little further down, but it was stuck.

'Aaargh!' he cried out in frustration. The wind was screaming past his ears, and the rain ferociously beat at his face and head like an assailant.

Suddenly, he saw something moving through the water, something small, pink and fleshy-looking and grabbing the prop for extra support, he leaned forward to get a better view.

A hand the size of a small child's broke the water and reached for him. In alarm he pulled back, using the prop to steady himself as he did so. All of a sudden the prop broke free, leaving the hook embedded in the branch. He slid off the board he was kneeling on and into the river, plunging head first into the icy, turbulent waters. An impromptu gasp at the shock of the cold forced him to take in water

He blindly grabbed for the branch, tearing his hand on the thread of the hook. A sharp piece of debris broke away from the dam, cutting him deeply above the eye. As the water filled his mouth, he could feel a burning sensation in his throat. He felt a little lightheaded and the sensation was not unpleasant, but all of his senses were keen and he knew the river wasn't too deep at that point especially with the dam holding back the flow. He only had to try and find a footing on the bed and grab hold of the dam, and he would be able to make his way over to the bank.

He tried to stand but couldn't. Something had hold of him. Something was grabbing his leg,

A Strange Encounter at Little Hubery

trying to keep his head under. He panicked and kicked out wildly, his heart hammering in his chest, the roaring of the water deafening in his ears. He lashed out once more and felt something give, and suddenly he was free. He struggled to find his feet, slipping on the slimy mud and plant life on the riverbed before gaining a firmer footing. He gasped for air and coughed, spitting out the foul-tasting muddy water in his mouth. He wiped blood from the gash above his eye and grabbed hold of a solid chunk of wood wedged firmly between the banks. Using it as a handrail, he made his way to the bank. It would have been closer and easier for him to climb out on the left bank closer to home and he looked longingly up at the house, but he knew he had to get back to the station. He could not and would not abandon his stranded passengers.

He reached the right bank and clambered out, his progress slow and difficult. When he'd reached firmer ground, he rolled onto his back and gasped for air, his breathing laboured, his chest tight and painful. The cut above his eye was throbbing and his hand was stinging. He had quite badly banged one knee when he fell, but other than that he was none the worse for wear. He lay back for a while until his breathing eased, and he stared up at the sky, moonless and angry. A loud clap of thunder rang out and a flash of lighting was quick to follow. The lightening forked and he heard a bang as though something nearby had been struck. He managed to sit upright, and he saw with surprise that the dam had collapsed. Lying on his stomach, he reached out and managed to grab some of the shattered pieces, throwing them wide to avoid them jamming up again. He reached for the last big chunk of wood when something caught his eye. A tiny glove, a child's glove, pink, dirty and sodden, had floated upstream towards him and was caught on a clod on the bank. He shuddered and tried to push all thoughts that it was crawling up the bank towards him firmly out of his mind.

Chapter Fifteen

'Dear God man, what happened to you?' barked Sir Gregory as Arthur almost fell through the waiting room door.

Arthur put up a hand to reassure them as the two women, the professor and the soldier came running to meet him, their eyes wide with concern.

'Oh look at his eye!' cried Ellen.

'I'm fine. I'm fine really,' said Arthur. 'The bridge was out and the debris had formed a dam. I fell in trying to clear it so the goods sheds wouldn't flood.'

'Why, my dear fellow,' said the professor. 'Why didn't you ask one of us for help?'

'Really I'm fine,' said Arthur, embarrassed by all the attention. 'I have fresh clothes in my office. If you'll excuse me I'll dry off there and change.'

He limped into his office and made up a good fire from the idling embers. After removing his clothes and checking for cuts and bruises, he bathed his eye and hand and patched them up with dressings from his first aid kit. The cut above his eye should really be stitched, he concluded, but for now this would have to do.

He dressed into fresh, dry clothes and was about to take a nip of whiskey to keep the cold at bay when a piercing scream from next door sent him running into the waiting room.

There in the middle of the floor with her head on her husband's knee lay Lady Agnes. She had fainted.

The waiting room had been quiet again. Sir Gregory was engrossed in a crossword, the professor seemed to be sleeping, and the soldier was wrapped in his own thoughts. The two ladies had sat together in silence, comforted by the close proximity to one another. Arthur of course was next door, changing in his office. Travers stood up and walked around the waiting room to stretch his legs. Robert watched him from his seat. There was something shifty about

A Strange Encounter at Little Hubery

the man he couldn't quite put his hand on. Travers sat down beside Ellen and began to speak in hushed tones.

'Oh!' said Ellen. Travers stood up with a smile, and the soldier watched him as Travers made his way to his seat. A loud clap of thunder overhead made everyone jump and woke the professor with a start. Lady Agnes was all of a sudden very cold, and she pulled her coat tightly around her shoulders. She had the feeling she was being watched and looked nervously around the room, noticing how quiet everything had become.

A flash of lightening made her look toward the window where a shadowy figure stood out on the platform looking in, the figure of a man, a tall man. Just a silhouette against a bleached-out background, and then the lightning faded away to nothing. Lady Agnes could just make out a face, a pale haunted face that stared straight back at her, only dark shadows where his eyes should be. She froze, certain that her heart would stop in terror. She closed her eyes tight and prayed silently, her quivering mouth forming words that no-one else could hear. When she opened her eyes again, the figure had vanished and that's when she screamed and fell to the floor in a dead faint. Her husband and Ellen ran to her aid. The professor stood up in alarm. From the dark chimney corner, Robert heard a low snigger.

'What did he say to you?' he demanded of Ellen, striding past the prostrate figure of Lady Agnes. 'What did that creature say to you?'

Ellen gasped.

'I really don't think this is the right time,' added the professor. 'Poor Lady Agnes, is she…'

Suddenly Arthur came into the room and saw Lady Agnes on the floor. By this time she was stirring, moaning as she regained consciousness. She looked up at the people crowded around her.

'Give her room,' said Arthur. 'She's fainted, she needs air.'

Lady Agnes had recovered her wits, and her eyes widened with fear as she grabbed her husband's arm tightly.

'The man,' she jabbered. 'On the platform. He stared in at me, but…He-he had no eyes. Oh Gregory it was awful. Awful!' She started to sob and Gregory put a protective arm around his

A Strange Encounter at Little Hubery

wife to comfort her. Arthur ran to the door to check outside on the platform and Robert made to follow him when Ellen grabbed his arm forcefully.

Both looked towards the shadowy chimney corner, where only the bottom of Travers' legs and feet were visible. Then Ellen turned to Robert, her eyes aglow in the light of the fire.

'What did he say to you, Miss?' Robert said, his face set hard. Ellen looked up at him, at his ruggedly handsome face, at his wide jaw and his deep set eyes. He reminded her of Humphrey Bogart.

'He told me…' said Ellen, jumping as the fire spit with a loud crack. 'He told me that the station was haunted.'

A Stranger's Tale

His fiancée had never looked so beautiful. He watched her with a warm feeling inside as she sipped her tea and chattered excitedly about flowers and rings…and honeymoons. A frown crossed his face at the thought of the cost of his beloved's perfect wedding, but she was too preoccupied to notice.

He thought how happy she looked with her shining eyes and her incessant giggles, and he knew then that he would do anything to make her dreams come true. With a deep sigh, he left her to her society magazines and her afternoon tea, kissed her lightly on the cheek and with a heavy heart, walked over to his work at the bank.

Nervous Norman, fidgety as ever, had been pacing the banking hall looking for him when he returned. Mrs Baxter was waiting for him, and she would see no-one else. He smiled, knowing the cantankerous old dear had a soft spot for

A Strange Encounter at Little Hubery

him, also knowing that she would be adding to her immense wealth by depositing into her account. He had been siphoning the odd copper from several of his wealthier clientele for the past few months now and transferring into his own account. A few bob here and there, never enough to be missed. But so far, probably due to her fondness for him, he'd avoided doing so to Mrs Baxter's account, even though she was one of the richest people in town.

His was a pretty, little town, close to the sea with far-reaching views and surrounded by farmland and lush green fields. It was a haven for the retired wealthy of Harrogate and York, and with many of London's elite having their country pile close by, he had his choice of rich pickings.

Mrs Baxter, who'd received a substantial amount after the death of her late husband in an industrial accident, was also in benefit of a tidy pension each week. Add this to rent she received from various inherited properties, and Mrs Baxter was a very wealthy lady indeed. In fact that very afternoon she was in town to deposit a cheque for the substantial amount of one hundred and two pounds, two pounds of which found its way into the account of her favourite bank clerk.

Chapter Sixteen

'Bloody ghosts!' snapped Arthur. 'That's all we need when people are shook up already. What's the fellow thinking of?'

'I'm not sure,' replied Robert angrily. 'But someone needs to have a word.'

'Hmm! Right now I'm more concerned about a trespasser on railway property.'

The two men were searching the station looking for Lady Agnes' ghost. Even after a shot of brandy and a hot sweet tea, she stood by her conviction. There was no doubt in her mind whatsoever that the creature that watched her from the platform was 'not of this world.' Her husband, over the shock of her little fainting spell, had scoffed and ridiculed the notion. The professor, a man of science, had attempted to convince the ladies, for Ellen too had remained unsettled, that there was no scientific evidence as to the existence of spirits and that there was no evidence whatsoever to suggest that the man on the platform was anything but a prowler, looking for shelter from the storm.

Ellen kept looking around nervously at the man in the corner, and although his face was in shadow, she was certain he was grinning at her. She shuddered and went over to the window to look for the men returning. She hoped it would be soon. Travers gave her the creeps, and she held little faith in the abilities of the professor and Sir Gregory to protect the ladies in case of an emergency.

Finally Arthur and Robert returned, perplexed and a little uneasy. There was no one to be found on or around the station, and unless you had keys to the outbuildings, which only Arthur had (a spare set living in the booking office), there was nowhere to hide unless you ran along the tracks, and only a fool would do so. No, they were convinced the figure had been the result of an overwrought lady with a vivid imagination, neither man conceding their true thoughts on the matter but both willing to admit that Lady Agnes had struck them as neither overwrought or given to fits of fancy.

A Strange Encounter at Little Hubery

It was decided in light of recent happenings that no one was to go outside alone and that the ladies would use the staff facilities in pairs. The doors were locked and Robert, Arthur and Travers (whom the soldier kept a good eye on) took it in turns to patrol the station buildings. After another hot drink laced with a tot, the three elders dozed off to the dreamy sounds of Al Bowelly. Sir Gregory snored softly and from the way Lady Agnes cried out occasionally, it was obvious her sleep was troubled.

Ellen remained uneasy and kept looking over at Robert, who gave her a reassuring smile from time to time. Arthur kept looking at his knee which guaranteed to be stiff and bruised come morning.

The storm seemed to be passing over; only the occasional flicker of lightning illuminated the waiting room windows, making diamonds of the raindrops on the glass. The wind had died down too, but the steady patter of rain persisted and Arthur was worried about the extent of the damage the storm had wrought.

Ellen felt her eyelids growing heavy and could hardly keep them from closing. She had barely nodded off when a strange mewling sound from by the fire woke her up. It was Sir Gregory; he was whimpering and moaning in his sleep and seemed very distressed. Lady Agnes, by his side was also roused by her husband's noise. Only the professor slept on unawares.

Sir Gregory's face was bathed in sweat, and beneath his tightly closed lids his eyes darted about in rapid succession. He was mumbling something now, repeating himself over and over, his voice getting louder as he thrashed about in his seat.

'No!' he cried out. 'No it's not true. He deserved to hang…He was guilty, I tell you, guilty…'

'Gregory. Gregory dear, wake up. You're dreaming. Wake up.' His wife shook his shoulder gently, afraid to startle him, but he wouldn't wake.

'I'm sorry,' said his wife to the others. 'He's been doing this lately. He's been under a lot of stress, what with the trial and all. I'm really sorry.'

All of a sudden, the old man's eyes snapped open, bleary but wide and full of fear. His wife

A Strange Encounter at Little Hubery

was full of concern, but she also looked embarrassed and irritated by the spectacle.

'Gregory, you've been dreaming again,' she chided. 'You really should see a doctor.'

'Don't be ridiculous woman. Since when did a dream ever harm anyone?' he snapped.

Lady Agnes looked at her husband coldly and the others looked away, embarrassed to have witnessed the quarrel between husband and wife. All but Travers, who called out from his corner.

'Interesting case that, Sir Gregory.' All eyes turned to the disembodied voice in the darkened corner. Travers stepped out of the shadows, the unnervingly smug grin never leaving his face.

'What? What's that?' puffed the old man. His wife looked at him sharply and the professor noticed a look of alarm flicker in her eyes.

'I was in the public gallery that day sir. That day you donned your sentencing cap and sealed that poor idiot boy's fate....*Sir!*

'What impertinence is this, my good fellow?' bellowed the judge. 'I suggest you sit down sir, before I'm forced to take my belt to you.'

Robert stood up, ready to lunge at Travers, who calmly walked up and stood behind Ellen's seat, holding on to the backrest with both hands. If he was afraid of a beating, he certainly didn't show it. Ellen visibly shuddered at the close proximity.

'The kidnapping of that society boy, all of six he was,' the man continued, moving around closer, his eyes never leaving the judge, who stared back incredulously. 'His mother was never allowed to identify his little body. Or what was left of it…'

Lady Agnes looked at Travers in horror. Ellen stifled a sob.

'Why you…' said Robert, moving closer to the man.

'Animal,' roared Sir Gregory, red in the face and panting with exertion. 'The boy's father paid that scoundrel his ransom demands and still he tore that poor child limb from limb.'

'Oh!' cried out Lady Agnes, burying her face in her hands.

'And yet we're meant to believe that a simple stable hand engineered the whole thing? That he single-handedly hatched an ingenious, untraceable kidnap plot, stole the boy away from home…'

A Strange Encounter at Little Hubery

'Really this is too much,' said the professor, but Travers continued undeterred.

'That he calculated a ransom, tactically arranged a drop-off so the police couldn't find him, callously murdered a child he had known since birth, and then calmly went back to the working in the stables at the parents home, even though he was now rich beyond his wildest dreams?'

Sir Gregory seemed to have shrunk back into himself. He seemed to find it hard to gather his words.

'It was because the boy knew him, see?' he said imploringly to Arthur. 'That's how he was able to lead him away.' He turned to the professor 'The boy trusted him,' he said grabbing the professor's arm.

The judge was sweating now. He turned to look at the faces of the people around him, a sea of faces, and he felt as though he was drowning, finding it hard to breathe.

'That's enough now,' said Arthur authoritatively, grabbing Travers' arm. Travers pulled away with a strength that amazed Arthur.

'Besides,' whimpered Sir Gregory, barely audibly, 'the boy's bloodied shoe was found in the stables. The evidence was irrefutable.'

'The evidence was planted by a corrupt and incompetent police force who knew there would be a public outcry if no-one was brought to trial for this atrocity,' said Travers calmly. 'You knew, Sir Gregory. You knew this and you buried it. You knew witnesses for the defence were being intimidated and you did nothing.'

'Stop it!' groaned his wife. 'Please stop it.'

'LIES!' screamed the judge, standing and roughly pushing his accuser away. 'All lies, damn you!' He shook a finger in Travers' face. His eyes were bloodshot and his lip was trembling. 'You've no proof of this sir, I tell you. No proof!' He walked away from the group, towards the back of the room and down the corridor that led to the staff conveniences.

All turned and watched him go.

'Michael Turner was an innocent man Sir Gregory! A scapegoat,' said Travers sadly. 'You sent a poor, simple-minded, innocent man to the gallows.'

Chapter Seventeen

Little Hubery station stood isolated and alone on a sodden and storm-tossed moorland landscape. Its flickering fire-lit windows stood out like a beacon on the dark and desolate heath.

Cut off from civilisation by the raging storm, five strangers sat in silence. The sixth, Sir Gregory, had not yet returned from the bathroom after his altercation with the man Travers.

Each one of them was lost in his or her own thoughts, cut off from one another by a deep brooding introspection that hovered over them like a poisonous cloud. An external entity that bored its way into the mind, leaving suggestions, just a seed of an idea that germinated and grew into a dark and worrisome cognizance.

Robert was thinking, what the hell was that, and how and why had it come about? He looked across at Travers and wondered about the strange and unpleasant man. Why suddenly turn against the judge like that? He was no fan of the pompous old fool himself, less so if the accusations against him were true, but why had he been held to trial like that? An ironic turnabout for a magistrate. Travers had barely spoken two words to anyone all night and now this! It was a strange business.

Travers, who hadn't moved since sitting back in his seat, abruptly turned his head towards Robert, who could feel his eyes boring into him, even though the other man's face was hidden by shadows. Robert could feel his flesh creeping as though something were crawling on his skin, inside his clothes.

There was a strange, unpleasant atmosphere in the waiting room, and he was sure it was emanating from Travers. Robert remembered how he'd felt out there, exposed on the moor. How vulnerable he'd felt. He never wanted to feel that way again.

He stood and lit a cigarette and walked over to the fire. He could see Ellen watching him out of the corner of his eye and he offered around

A Strange Encounter at Little Hubery

his cigarettes. Only she accepted and came and joined him by the hearth.

Lady Agnes was thinking, he couldn't know that, he simply couldn't! What was the wretched man's idea? Was it some kind of blackmail plot? Was it his intention to bring her husband down? Defame him? Maybe he was someone Gregory had previously sent to the gaol, or the family member of someone he'd sent to the gaol. Perhaps he was related to that poor soul he'd sent to the gallows. But how could he know about the evidence? Why here, and now? How did he know they would be here? How could he? Had he followed them? At that last thought she began trembling uncontrollably. The professor sat next to her looked at her with concern.

'Oh dear, where is my husband?' she said out loud.

Ellen studied Robert's face in profile. The light from the fire cast deep shadows and made his features seem all the more rugged and chiselled. Completely the opposite of George, she thought, fair, quiet and bookish. The soldier, Robert was dark and mysterious. If only she knew what was troubling this handsome stranger. She watched as he drew from his cigarette, causing the end to glow like a headlamp. She found herself wondering whether he was married. She found herself wondering whether that would make a difference. Hidden among the shadows in the darkened chimney corner, Travers smiled.

Arthur tried to phone Shearing's Vale to see whether there was any progress, but it seemed the storm had brought the phone lines down. Only the same bizarre static he'd heard earlier on the wireless came from the instrument. He placed the receiver back onto its cradle and sat on the edge of his desk, rubbing his eyes.

'Oh let this night be over,' he groaned. 'Let it be over.' He thought of what had just happened and how strange the man Travers was. Earlier, whilst checking out the station buildings, Arthur learned a little about the soldier Robert and how he had finished serving in India and was to be stationed at Catterick. He'd had a good

A Strange Encounter at Little Hubery

conversation with the girl Ellen about how she was to be a department head in a girls' school in Northumberland while the two of them made tea, and about Sir Gregory everyone was already familiar. Besides his wife Lady Agnes had been pleasant and talkative for most of the evening. The professor, they'd learned he was unmarried and lived in Saltburn and was travelling home from visiting friends in Cambridge, but about Travers they knew nothing. He had made no attempts to communicate nor offered any information about himself to anyone. Very odd, thought Arthur, very, very odd.

He was feeling the beginnings of a bad headache and rubbed the top of his nose with his forefinger and thumb. At least the storm is calming somewhat... in fact it's almost too quiet! he mused. He stood and was about to make for the door when the phone sprang into life, it shrill ringing deafening in the lull of the storm.

'Bloody hell!' he exclaimed, then 'Oh, thank God for small mercies.'

'Little Hubery. Stationmaster McLaren speaking.' Static, a voice barely discernable, more static and then...

'Arthur? Arthur…'

'Hello. Hello? Yes?' Suddenly his blood ran cold as a low snigger could be heard over the phone and the same voice he'd heard on the wireless croaked…

'Before this night ends…'

Chapter Eighteen

Sir Gregory washed his face and looked at himself in the mirror. His heart was racing and he had a pain across his shoulder. His breath was laboured and fear held him in its grasp.

'Damned fellow,' he cursed. To attack him like that, in front of his wife, in front of all those people. Why if he were twenty years younger, he'd thrash the scoundrel to within an inch of his life. What did he hope to achieve? He felt a darkness creep into his mind, crawling, probing, seeking out his deepest thoughts and memories, searching for and merging with the darkness in his very soul. His thoughts turned to murder, to power, to the power he held in silencing this filth that sought to challenge him, to expose him. He was a powerful man, a man of some influence. Who did this lowlife think he was? Sir Gregory winced as a pain shot up his arm and his chest tightened.

'Lies!' he screamed at his reflection. 'All lies!'

Who was he to challenge the chief of police? He held no power over the force and what they did and didn't do. So what if they had tampered with the evidence? How was that his fault? He could only work with what he had... the evidence against the boy was overwhelming...if he *was* innocent then...

A sudden movement among the shadows at the back of the room caught his attention. He wiped his face on the towel and made to turn around when something drew him to the mirror. Over his left shoulder he could see a figure, that of a young man, wiry and strong with foppish dark hair. The figure was looking down at the ground, and the judge found himself unable to move. Paralysed with fear, unable to tear himself away from the reflection of the boy who was even now raising his head to meet him eye to eye, Sir Gregory wheezed and fought for breath. Beads of sweat covered his forehead and ran down the back of his neck. He felt he was burning even though the room was icy cold. His legs refused to support him and he managed to grab the edge of the sink for support.

A Strange Encounter at Little Hubery

The boy's face was in full view now and the judge closed his eyes tightly. He didn't need to look. He already knew that the shade of Michael Turner, the innocent boy he had sent to the gallows, was here to exact his deadly revenge. A tear squeezed its way from between his tightly closed lids, and he knew he would have to meet Turner's ghost face to face, man to man.

If he expected rattling chains and lamentations then the judge was mistaken, for the shade of Michael Turner stood before him now as it had done in life. The look of terror he had last worn was replaced by sadness and melancholy. Dark rings circled his eyes and his lips and cheek were bloodless, almost translucent. He wore the clothes he was hanged in and he never once took his eyes off Sir Gregory.

'What do you want of me spirit?' Gregory asked with the false bravado of Scrooge when faced with Marley's ghost. The boy's lips moved but no words came out. He opened his mouth wide and it was cavernous, empty and black, without tongue or teeth. The judge felt as though he were being pulled in, as though his soul were being sucked from him, and then as suddenly as he had appeared, the spirit was gone.

Sir Gregory sank to his knees and somehow managed to pull his legs around so his back rested against the pedestal of the sink. He no longer felt the pain in his chest, and his breathing seemed to have eased. He felt as though he were floating, no longer grounded. He could hear sounds around him. In fact he could hear someone calling out to him, pounding on the bathroom door, which he was certain wasn't locked, but all the sounds were distant, as if muted by time.

He heard from the corner of the room a strange sound, like a death rattle in someone's throat, and then a snigger. He felt numb but no longer cold or hot, and he could see the shadows moving before his eyes. He heard his own voice cry out guilty, but it didn't come from within. He could make out movement from the darkest corner and his eyes bulged with terror at the sight before him. Once more, he struggled for breath. His throat felt constricted, his windpipe crushed and his tongue lolled lifelessly from his mouth. He felt the hot liquid run down his inner thigh and heard the sound of a gavel hitting a sounding block. The last thing Sir Gregory ever saw was the lipless mouth of the hanging carcass grinning at him from the corner of the room.

Chapter Nineteen

Professor Victor Rose walked with some apprehension down the darkened corridor toward the staff conveniences. Not easily given to tales of ghosts and ghouls and things that go bump in the night, he had to admit to feeling rather spooked, what with the storm, the wild moorland setting, talk of prowlers and now this...this creepy man Travers. What was his game? he wondered, and what was the meaning of that outburst? Could his accusations be true? Sir Gregory had clearly been shaken by it.

He was going at the request of Lady Agnes to check on the judge. Her husband had been gone awhile and she was getting worried. The professor, normally a level-headed man of science, crossed his fingers and hoped for no more unpleasant surprises that night.

When he reached the door, a sudden feeling of apprehension came over him and he paused

A Strange Encounter at Little Hubery

for a moment, his fingertips rested lightly on the door. He put his ear against the panel and listened. He could hear faint murmurs of conversation from the other passengers in the waiting room. Arthur was in his office, talking on the telephone, and Professor Rose could see a chink of light beneath the office door. From within the staff toilet all was quiet, but shadows moving beneath the door told the professor that Barnes was moving about.

'Sir Gregory?' The professor tapped gently on the door and then knocked a little louder. 'Sir Gregory, are you alright? Your wife is quite concerned about you.' He pushed against the door but it wouldn't budge. Strange, he thought to himself, I don't remember the outer door having a lock!

'Sir Gregory, could you open the door please?' From inside he thought he heard laughter, deep and rasping. He pushed the door firmly but it held fast.

'Sir Gregory, please. If you can hear me, open the door.' The professor spoke a little louder, but not loud enough to cause concern to the judge's wife, sitting in the waiting room. He put his shoulder against the door and applied some force, but it still refused to move. He could hear Sir Gregory talking to someone and wondered if he'd caught the prowler. The thought left the professor cold, and he shook the door so hard that the doorknob rattled. Suddenly the talking stopped and he stood back to gain momentum when all at once the door of the stationmaster's offer swung open.

'Arthur,' the professor hissed at the surprised man. 'The key for this door, do you have it? Sir Gregory is trapped inside.'

'That door doesn't lock,' said the stationmaster with a puzzled expression. 'It's recently planed, it doesn't even stick.'

'Then please,' cried Professor Rose, 'help me open it.' Arthur grabbed the doorknob and gave it a twist. It turned easily and the door swung open. The two men looked at each other in bewilderment for a moment and then rushed inside. There, leant against the pedestal of the sink, sprawled Sir Gregory. His jaw drooped and his tongue hung from between blue lips like a piece of dead meat on a butcher's hook. His wide, sightless eyes fixed into the darkened cubicle corner where the shadows from the gas lamp seemed to vanish into the impenetrable

A Strange Encounter at Little Hubery

blackness of the deepest recesses. His pupils were dilated so only the tiniest rim of flecked grey iris showed. Sir Gregory was dead.

'Good Lord,' gasped the professor. 'Look at his face!'

'God help us,' Arthur said, quickly looking away. He turned to the professor and his face was deadly serious. 'It looks to me as though this man died of fright!'

Back in the waiting room Arthur, the professor and Robert stood deep in conversation, their faces grave. Above the hushed exchange, the occasional sob rang out from Lady Agnes, who was being given brandy and comforted by an equally distressed Ellen; the latter kept looking up at the men nervously. Sir Gregory's body had been removed to a small filing room at the back of the building and covered with a blanket. Arthur had attempted unsuccessfully to use the phone, and Travers had been ordered not to leave his seat. The wireless was playing 'Sailing By' prior to the shipping forecast and Ellen moved to turn it off.

'Leave it on dear,' sniffed Lady Agnes, dabbing her eyes with a lace handkerchief. 'It comforts me.'

'What if the man died as a direct result of Travers' confrontation?' said Robert.

'We can't possibly know that,' replied Arthur. 'Besides it looks for all intents and purposes as if he had a heart attack…'

'But the expression on his face,' cut in the professor. 'It was a look of sheer terror!'

'And Travers never left his seat,' Arthur said. 'He was nowhere near the man when he died. True he may have challenged Sir Gregory. Undoubtedly he upset him. But to have brought about his death? He wasn't even aggressive toward him. He's done nothing wrong. We would be breaking the law if we attempted to accost him in any way.'

The soldier sighed and turned angrily towards the chimney corner before looking back.

'So what do you suggest then, stationmaster?' he asked coldly. 'We are all

A Strange Encounter at Little Hubery

holed up here with tales of ghosts and prowlers abounding and then there's this, this creature…'

'Please lower your voice sir. We don't want to upset the ladies any more than they are already,' said the professor. 'He is a little odd I agree, but Arthur's right. We can't go locking him up against his will. Better we all stick together and keep an eye on him.'

Arthur gathered everyone around. Five weary travellers with pale faces and bloodshot eyes sat huddled around the fire. In the amber glow Ellen's eyes were wide with fear, while Lady Agnes' glistened with unshed tears. The soldier and the professor were silent. Even Travers was respectfully subdued, although Robert was certain he saw a trace of mockery in his eyes. Or maybe it was just the firelight. He rubbed his own tired eyes and caught Ellen smiling at him from the seat opposite. He never returned her smile, turning instead to look at Arthur. The stationmaster cleared his throat.

'Ladies and gentlemen, we had all suffered a terrific shock tonight and I'm sure our thoughts and condolences lie with Lady Agnes.' Ellen rubbed the old lady's shoulder and Sir Gregory's widow smiled her thanks at those gathered.

'The loss of Sir Gregory is indeed tragic and in such *forced* circumstances. However having thoroughly examined the, the, err, gentleman concerned, Professor Rose, Lance Corporal Newton and myself are quite convinced that there are no signs of trauma to the body and that Sir Gregory died of entirely natural causes.'

Ellen glared at Travers, who met her stare and refused to look away. For a moment she found herself unable to break his stare, mesmerised by the bottomless depths of those pale, colourless eyes. She had never seen eyes so deep and yet so empty. It was as though they lacked humanity, they were soulless! She eventually pulled away and shuddered. She suddenly felt violated. It was as though he had been inside her mind and could see her deepest, darkest secrets. She attempted to shake off the feeling, but it stayed with her. She tried to concentrate on what Arthur was saying, but she could hear Travers' voice in her head, calling her…

A Strange Encounter at Little Hubery

Unable to stop herself, her eyes met his and locked. Arthur's words were faint, like background noise. All she could hear was Travers. Travers putting thoughts into her head, rooting out her own thoughts and taunting her with them. Reminding her of George, of how his touch made her feel, of the dirty things they did together after work. Of how she had imagined Robert and her, naked, writhing together, his big manly hands on her body, touching her in that special place…

Arthur's voice cut through the mist like a scythe through wheat, bringing her abruptly back to the present. She felt warm and damp like she'd been touched, and she crossed her legs and blushed deeply.

'We did have a prowler on the premises earlier,' said the stationmaster. 'Likely someone looking for shelter from the storm, but he is long gone. The incident with the wireless, the static was surely down to the storm. We are all a little tired and are susceptible to influences that we wouldn't normally take mind of, but I can assure you we are quite safe in the station. I am hopeful that we will all be home and in our beds within the hour…'

A sob from Lady Agnes silenced him.

Chapter Twenty

'Guilt, gentlemen...and lady,' said Lady Agnes, smiling graciously at Ellen, 'is a terrible burden and my husband, God rest his soul, stood guilty as charged.' The others stared at Lady Agnes as if she'd gone mad and the professor opened his mouth to speak, but the old lady held up a hand as if to stop him.

'The gentleman here, Mr Travers, was right in the accusation he made against my husband. Gregory knew there'd been a cover-up and he held his tongue. He knew the public were baying for blood, and he sent that poor young man to the gallows knowing that the kidnapper or kidnappers would go free. Oh, the young stable hand was involved alright. He led the kidnapper to the boy. But he was a simple-minded fellow who doted on the child, so one can assume that whatever part he played in the crime, he did so unwittingly.' She sniffed and dabbed her eyes before carrying on.

'The chief of police and Gregory were friends of old. They went to college together, and Thomas and his wife were guests at both our wedding and our son's christening. Anyhow when Thomas came to Gregory and told him how the evidence had been tampered with and how his reputation and livelihood were at stake if the kidnapper wasn't brought to justice, Gregory begged him to set things straight, it wasn't too late! He even threatened to halt the trial.'

'So what happened?' said Robert, sitting forward in his chair.

'My husband was a very loyal man, Lance Corporal. When Thomas told him he had no other choice, I'm afraid Gregory felt he had to stand by him. The police were convinced Mr Turner was involved in some way, but they knew he couldn't be the one who'd kidnapped the child.'

'What?' said Robert, the disgust and disbelief evident in his voice. Lady Agnes looked up at the professor for support, but he lowered his head. She carried on sadly.

A Strange Encounter at Little Hubery

'It's not known whether Mr Turner inadvertently allowed the kidnappers onto the property or whether he was tricked into taking the boy to them.' She sighed. 'It was clear however that he had no idea as to his involvement with the 'kidnapper' or where his actions would lead.'

'Dear God!' cried Ellen, biting her fist. The old lady continued.

'Michael Turner was, as Mr Travers had said, a poor simpleton, an innocent scapegoat. The police had no further leads as to the kidnapper's identity, and Mr Turner was a poor witness, unable to supply any clues or put forward any clear descriptions. When the beast sent the police the boy's shoe…' She sobbed unable to continue, and the professor offered her his handkerchief.

'When the kidnapper sent the boy's shoe to the chief of police he, he planted it in the stable where Mr Turner worked, and one day a call came in to the boy's parents from the kidnapper while the stable hand was in the kitchen with the house-keeper. The house-keeper reported this to the police at the time, but was told to stay silent, that she would be suspected as an accomplice if she got involved. I'm sure the family and their staff doubted Mr Turner's guilt. After all, they'd known him as a child. His father was a much-loved and loyal member of the household staff, and everyone knew that Michael adored the little chap. But the public were baying for blood and it seemed the police had their man.'

'Incredible!' said Arthur suddenly jumping up. 'So Travers was right after all. But Lady Agnes, why didn't you do something about it?'

'What could she do, go to the police?' scoffed Travers. 'Besides, what use was this information after the man had hanged? Lady Agnes couldn't have known until then. The law forbids discussing the details of an ongoing case with anyone.'

'I didn't,' sobbed the old lady. 'I didn't know and now not only have I lost my husband, I will have to live with this for the rest of my life.' She cried as if her heart would break, and Ellen stood up to comfort her.

'What we have learned tonight must not leave this room,' said the professor. 'Lady Agnes has suffered enough and as for—for the judge!' he said, unable to bring himself to use his name, 'be sure his own judgement day is at

A Strange Encounter at Little Hubery

hand. He is beyond reproach. There is nothing to be gained from taking this any further.'

'Sir Gregory Barnes, KC,' scoffed Robert.

'Let him without sin cast the first stone, *Lance Corporal*!' said Travers, coolly eyeing the soldier. Robert turned on him angrily.

'And you, Travers, if that be your name at all! How come you have so much inside knowledge about the case?' All eyes turned to the man suspiciously. 'The only way you could know such things is if you were directly involved, say a member of the force…*or the kidnapper!*' Ellen gasped and the three men tensed as if ready to strike. If Travers was intimidated, he didn't show it.

'Quite a temper you have there, Lance Corporal.' He smirked at the soldier. 'But I'm sorry to disappoint you. You see I couldn't have committed the evil deed. Rather like your good self sir, I was in India when the Haughton boy was kidnapped!'

Lady Agnes suddenly felt unburdened, almost cheerful. She refused to feel guilty about this. She refused to feel guilty about anything anymore. After all, she'd done nothing wrong.

In the wake of the hanging, her husband had hid his culpability well. The way he casually spoke of the case, it was as though he'd talked himself into believing Turner's guilt. Maybe that was the only way he could live with himself. It was then she'd become aware that she didn't really love Gregory and probably never had. If she had been guilty of anything, then she had served her sentence, and with Gregory's death came release. She didn't care if the others judged her. She didn't care what anyone thought. After years of living with a domineering, tyrannical man, she was free. She dabbed away an imaginary tear, the professor's handkerchief hiding the widow's inopportune smile.

Ellen was still in shock. She would never have suspected the judge of such a foul deed. People's souls were indeed a deep well of dark secrets. An image of George's wife suddenly crept into her mind and she quickly swept it away. She looked towards the darkened chimney corner and then looked away. She didn't care to dwell too long on thoughts of Travers and how he knew the things he knew.

A Strange Encounter at Little Hubery

Oh dear! thought Professor Rose. He just wanted to be home. He was unsettled by recent revelations, he was unsettled by the storm and being stranded in a isolated location, but most of all he had been unsettled by Travers. Sinister, cool, all-knowing Travers. Why it was almost as if he could read people's minds. And everyone had something to hide, didn't they?

Arthur's mind was somewhere else entirely. Could he risk walking up the track to the signal-box to find out if young Jack had any more news? How would his poor old dog Meg be faring alone in the house with the storm tearing around? Why, again, did this have to happen in his station? And how long did it take to clear a tree anyway?

Robert was quietly seething. He couldn't remember whether Travers had been in earshot when he'd told Arthur he'd been stationed in India, but he was certain he hadn't. One thing was for sure though, it was information in dangerous hands. What manner of creature was Travers anyway? How did he know so much? He wished for five minutes alone with the man.

He would thrash the information out of him. Robert nibbled nervously at his fingernails, while in the darkened corner a figure silently watched.

And what Travers was thinking was anyone's guess.

A Stranger's Tale

Seated at his desk, he could see the comings and goings of the entire banking hall. Nervous Norman, Mr Sykes the assistant manager, and Sir Henry Mullen the bank manager had been in covert meetings all morning. He'd had an uneasy feeling in the pit of his stomach all day but with a rehearsal later that evening, had put it down to pre-wedding jitters. Now he wasn't sure. Why so cloak and dagger? He was convinced he'd seen Norman giving him funny looks earlier, and Mr Sykes had actually said good morning to him for the first time in eight years, and that was really unusual!

Now with his bank account richer by a whole seventy-five pounds and thirteen shillings he was more than usually anxious. The cashiers were nervous too, whispering and speculating about the comings and goings of senior staff, but he very much doubted they had done anything they'd need to be worrying about.

Around three as they were preparing to close, Mr Sykes proclaimed there was to be an announcement made and could they all stay behind for five minutes. There were one or two groans from younger staff members who just wanted to be away after work, but a stern look from the assistant bank manager soon silenced them.

Preparing his end of day accounts, he gave a sigh of relief. So they weren't on to him after all! They'd never make an announcement over such matters. Now he was certain the rumours were true and that the announcement was to declare the impending retirement of Ernest Sykes and the promotion of nervous Norman. His relief was short-lived however, when unexpectedly it was Sir Henry's retirement that was announced, along with the appointment of Sykes as the new bank manager and Norman as his assistant.

Chapter Twenty-One

The rain was letting up a bit, but the wind had returned with a vengeance. All of the station's windows rattled in their boxes as it ripped across the moor emitting a strange howling noise. Outside was pitch-black now the lightning had abated, but the thunder still grumbled threateningly in the distance.

Lady Agnes was asleep on a bench in the far corner of the room, giving off gentle snores and seemingly peaceful. Robert was pacing in his stocking feet so as not to disturb the old lady and Ellen watched him, appreciative of his straight back and broad shoulders. Arthur was fetching coal, and the professor stood by the window watching the shadows play chase on the dimly lit platform.

'Strange kind of a storm this,' he said to no-one in particular. 'Seems to blow over, then turn round and come back. I'm sure I've seen nothing like it.'

Travers remained silent in his corner, his face in shadow. Ellen got up and began to fiddle with the wireless, finding a mellow station playing Ella Fitzgerald. She moved to the chair closest to the fire and watched the flames dance up the chimney back. She found herself feeling sleepy and closed her eyes for a moment. All at once she felt the icy cold fingers probing the inside of her mind and she knew instantly that it was Travers. Again she felt violated, like her most intimate feelings were being exposed, like this vile man was controlling her, prompting her thoughts and emotions but the feeling was overshadowed by visions of Robert and herself naked, in a heated clinch, flesh against flesh in a steamy embrace. Mouth finding mouth, tongues meeting…

Suddenly she snapped back to reality and ran over to the professor where he stood. Robert too had stopped pacing and came over and stood with them by the window. They all stared all one another incredulously and then it came again, seemingly across the wild moor, steaming through the night. The unmistakable sound of a train's whistle.

A Strange Encounter at Little Hubery

Arthur heard the noise from the coal store and came running in. Lady Agnes stirred in her sleep but did not awaken, Travers came forward from the shadows but did not stand with the others.

'It's a train,' said Ellen. 'Surely!'

'It's a train alright,' replied Arthur, making for the door. 'But something's wrong.' Ellen stared at the stationmaster, a feeling of dread rising in her stomach.

'What do you mean, something's wrong?' cried the professor. 'They're running trains again. We can all go home.'

'Listen,' said Robert. 'Arthur's right, something is terribly wrong.' They listened as the sounds got closer. Even the clunking of the side irons was discernible. 'Arthur how close is the nearest line approaching us from the west?

'There is no line approaching us from the west. The nearest east-west bearing line is over twenty mile away at Shearing's Vale.'

'It's just the sound carrying in the wind,' said Ellen. 'It's deceptive.'

Robert and the others followed Arthur onto the platform. Travers hovered in the doorway. Lady Agnes slept on.

'The wind's blowing from the east dear, off the sea.' the professor told Ellen gently. 'The train has to be coming from the north or the south.'

'But there are no signal lights, north or south,' said Arthur. 'That train is no more than a mile away, possibly less and coming towards us at great speed from the west over invisible tracks.'

'Oh no!' said Ellen backing into the doorway, her eyes wide with fear. 'No, no!'

'Even in the howling wind the train was loud enough to hear over a mile away,' said Arthur. 'Which is in itself strange. It must be almost upon us, running without signals and for all my years on the railway, I have never had a train run through my station when I haven't been aware of its approach long before it's visible to the naked eye.'

The soldier looked puzzled. 'What do you mean Arthur?'

'What I mean is, you can feel a train coming long before you see or even hear it. The tracks will warn of a train's approach a good while before the signal comes in. You can smell it, you can feel a vibration deep beneath your feet.

A Strange Encounter at Little Hubery

The whole atmosphere becomes charged with it.'

'But it is charged,' said the professor. 'Can't you feel it?'

The air *was* charged, with menace! It was as if an electrical current ran between them, infecting them with fear. The atmosphere was alive and it was nothing to do with the storm. All four stood frozen with fear as the phantom train hurtled invisibly towards them. Then all at once they saw it, shrouded in mist, the glow of the furnace on the footplate like the beam of a lighthouse on a foggy night. The train thundered past, contradictory to what they believed they had heard it was travelling north, along the track, but there was no-one on the footplate, likewise in the four well lit carriages it drew. The rush of air as it sped through almost knocked the three men back. Ellen was safe in the doorway of the waiting room. The smell of burning coal now filled the air and the train appeared for all intents and purposes as real to them as the station building itself. But as they stared after it as it disappeared into the distance, they saw with horror that the train wasn't running on the track at all, but a good foot above it. They stared, unable to look away until as quickly as it had appeared, the train simply melted away into the night. Not becoming a spec on the horizon as a real train would have done, but vanishing, dispersing into the enveloping darkness.

Ellen swayed unsteadily in the door, not noticing Travers holding up his arm to support her. The professor wiped rain and perspiration from his face, holding his hankie to his eyes as though he couldn't bear to see anymore. Robert's mouth felt dry, the need for a good stiff drink now imperative. Arthur stood silently at the very edge of the platform, staring into the distance as though the answer to the mystery of the disappearing train lay there.

Suddenly they heard a sound that froze the very blood in their veins—a sickening, bone crunching thud and then a piercing scream that filled the night. The wailing torturous scream of a woman, so loud and shrill that it hurt their ears. Robert ran forward to try to find the source, but Arthur grabbed his sleeve.

'We have to help her,' cried Robert struggling to be heard against the howling wind.

A Strange Encounter at Little Hubery

'There is no woman, 'said the professor wearily. 'It's an illusion.'

'And the train?' the soldier called out.

'An illusion,' said the professor, taking Ellen's hand and leading her gently back inside.

'All an illusion.' Robert followed him in and saw the old lady had awoken and was staring at them all with bleary-eyed confusion. He looked at the others and shook his head.

Only Arthur remained outside on the platform. The wind whipped at his face and the rain beat down, soaking his exposed head and running down the back of his collar. He stayed that way for a little while just staring into the night, into the darkness and along the twisting track that led to Clarings Brook and railway bridge three-sixty-one.

Chapter Twenty-Two

'But how can it be possible?' whispered Robert to the professor. Arthur had gone to his office to dry off and the ladies were visiting the bathroom.

'I mean, we all witnessed it.'

'We're all tired son,' said the professor kindly, his eyes rheumy, his face looking gaunt in the flickering light of the fire.

'We can't all have imagined it,' Robert cried and then lowered his voice. 'It was real. All of my senses told me so.'

'Mass hysteria,' ventured Travers from the corner. 'Sounds from out on the moor lent suggestion of an approaching train. Our tired minds and overwrought imaginations filled in the blanks.'

'Don't be ridiculous man,' sneered Robert. 'We all saw the same…'

'And how do you know we all saw the same, Lance Corporal?' said Travers, standing and

A Strange Encounter at Little Hubery

joining them by the fire. Robert looked at the man with disdain. 'I saw but a flashing light and felt an almighty gust of wind rushing by. And you Professor Rose?'

'I, I… I'm not so sure anymore. I could have sworn it was a train, but…'

'Seriously sir!' exclaimed Robert incredulously.

'I don't know,' said the professor 'I'm so tired and still in shock after the death of Sir Gregory and the revelation, but Travers is right, mass hysteria is a proven phenomenon. We can't even begin to unravel the complexities of the human mind Robert.' He sighed wearily.

'And you Travers,' snarled Robert. 'You seem to be an authority on most things. Who or what are you man?' Travers smiled pleasantly. He seemed to enjoy getting a rise out of the soldier.

'You could say I am a parapsychologist sir. I study and have a keen interest in anomalies, events that occur outside the boundaries of what we would perceive the 'norm.' I also have a fascination with the untapped potential of the human mind.'

'You mean you enjoy playing mind games,' scoffed the soldier. 'Like you did with the judge. How can anyone trust a word you say?'

'Let's not have hostility gentlemen, please,' sighed the professor. 'We have enough to contend with without this.'

The soldier glared at Travers, his rising anger palpable. The friction between the two men hung over them like a gathering of storm clouds, charged and heavy. Still, the mocking smile never left Travers' lips.

'The professor's right, Lance Corporal. We should make good what little time we have left in each others' company. Perhaps we could discuss our respective experiences of India?'

'Why you…' The soldier lunged at Travers, taking him by the lapels and driving him back against the chimney breast. His eyes were steely, narrow slits, his teeth gritted. He knew he was giving the man ammunition, but he was fuelled with rage as he pulled back to swing at the man in front of him.

'Gentlemen, please!' said Lady Agnes sharply. 'Ellen and I will not bear witness to such loutish behaviour.' The two ladies had returned from the bathroom and stood by the

A Strange Encounter at Little Hubery

corridor entrance glaring at the two men. Robert's hands dropped down by his side but he couldn't tear his eyes away from Travers, whose face lit up with triumph and whose mouth was twisted into a mocking leer. He had never once lost his composure, and Robert felt as though he were being toyed with.

'Come, Robert,' said Ellen leading him away. 'I'm making tea for everyone and I'll be grateful if you can help me carry it back.'

Robert and Ellen stood in the station's tiny kitchen. Ellen filled the kettle and prepared the teapot while Robert rinsed out the mugs. There was an uncomfortable silence between the two, Robert still silently fuming from his brush with Travers. Ellen tried to make small talk.

'I'll be glad to be home.' She smiled at the soldier. 'My aunt will be beside herself, and you, Robert, have you someone at home waiting for you?'

'My wife and daughter will be home,' said Robert noncommittally, not looking up from his task.

'Oh!' Ellen's heart sunk and she suddenly had a vision of Travers smirking in his corner.

As Robert passed Ellen the mugs, their fingers brushed. For a moment she looked into his eyes, but his expression was cold. She felt a sudden nausea and swayed. Robert grabbing her arm anxiously.

'Are you alright Ellen?' The concern was evident in his voice. Ellen fell into him, and for a moment he let her rest against his chest before holding her at arms length and uneasily studying her face.

'Just hold me, Robert,' she pleaded 'I'm so afraid.' Robert held her like a child, shuffling awkwardly as she pressed against him. Her hair brushed his face, and it smelled like apple. He could smell the lightly scented fragrance of her skin. He closed his eyes and inhaled deeply. In his arms Ellen trembled, her predatory smile hidden in the folds of his jacket.

From in the waiting room they heard a cry. Robert pushed Ellen away gently, glad of the release but apprehensive as to the nature of the disturbance. Passing the booking office, they

A Strange Encounter at Little Hubery

saw Arthur frantically looking through the contents of a drawer. He found what he was looking for and held up a set of keys. A puzzled frown marked his face.

'Arthur?'

Arthur jumped when the soldier spoke. He hadn't heard Ellen and Robert come in.

'Didn't you hear it?' he asked the bewildered pair. 'We all heard it! We were sat in the waiting room when we heard someone walking about in the corridor. The professor and myself went through to see who it was and…'

'There was nobody there,' finished Robert.

'No but the rear door was wide open and banging in the wind. I locked that door myself not ten minutes ago, I can swear to it. It was dark and I dropped the keys into the coal bucket and had to fumble around for them.'

'And you're certain the door was locked properly?'

Absolutely Miss,' said Arthur, noticing a strange flush on the girl's face. 'After tonight's little episode with the intruder, I double checked. I'm the only one who has the keys to the station. The spare set is locked away in this drawer…here.'

He waved both sets of keys at them.

'It's evident,' said the soldier, 'that someone's playing with us. The question is who…and why?'

Chapter Twenty-Three

After a full investigation of the station buildings and its surroundings had yielded nothing, six nervous strangers locked themselves into the waiting room and huddled by the fire. Lady Agnes had surprised all by suggesting a game of gin rummy at which she thrashed Arthur, the professor and Robert respectively. Robert paced restlessly, grumbling about his rumbling stomach and Travers seemed to be sleeping. It was clear that sleep was the last thing on the minds of the others, and the mugs of tea had been set aside in favour of whiskey and brandy courtesy of Arthur.

Ellen couldn't stop thinking of Robert and how he'd held her in the kitchen. She made her way over to the window and watched the angry, rolling clouds. She sighed. It seemed like they'd been in the waiting room forever, yet dawn seemed so far away. She felt nervous, apprehensive but strangely aroused and excited.

She knew there was more to come before this night was over. She hoped to have more time alone with the handsome soldier.

Outside was calm. The storm had abated but the clouds were heavy and menacing. The wind had caused havoc on the platform and everywhere was sodden and miserable. It was too dark to see past the opposite platform, though the moon was trying to break through the cloud cover. It suddenly reminded her of a poem.

> *'From the lightning in the sky*
> *As it passed me flying by,*
> *From the thunder and the storm,*
> *And the cloud that took the form*
> *When the rest of Heaven was blue*
> *Of a demon in my view.'*

'What's that dear?' said Lady Agnes. 'What are you saying? Speak up dear.'

'Oh!' said Ellen embarrassed. She turned to face them all, hand clutching her throat. She coloured. She hadn't realised she'd been speaking out loud.

A Strange Encounter at Little Hubery

'What is that, a poem?' said the soldier kindly, noticing her embarrassment. 'Is it one of yours? It's very good.'

Ellen mumbled, her throat suddenly parched.

'Alone,' said Travers, jumping out of the shadows and startling everyone. 'By Edgar Allen Poe. It's one of my favourites. Does it have fond connections for you too, Ms Potter?' He smiled at Ellen sympathetically and she slid into the nearest seat, covered her face and began to sob. The others rushed over to her in concern.

'I'm fine, seriously. I'm fine.' She smiled at Lady Agnes, who looked rather worried, and then she began to open up.

'George Sinclair and I worked together at a small grammar school in York. I taught classics and he was the history master.' Ellen sniffed and wiped her eyes before carrying on. 'And while George was not a man many would consider handsome, too thin, too studious and lacking even a modicum of humour, I loved him almost immediately.' She smiled. 'I loved his gentle manner and sad eyes, his strange sense of style and the way he blushed whenever I spoke to him…and I knew despite his being a married man, that he had feelings for me too.' She blushed and patted an imaginary tear from the corner of her eye. The others had left the warmth of the hearth and come to join her by the window.

'One particular night we were both working late in the library. It was getting dark early and although I lived but a stone's throw from the school, George insisted he see me home safely. I remember it was quite a nippy night, an early frost I believe, and I was quite ill-prepared for it, having only brought a lightweight jacket. Well George, being a gentleman, offered me his coat but I declined, opting rather to take his arm and snuggle up to keep warm.' She looked up at the expectant faces in the waiting room. Travers nodded as if to move her along.

'I was already besotted you see? And although I may not be in the first flushes of youth, I was quite unused to a gentleman's attention.' She paused and cleared her throat before continuing.

'My sister and I live close to the university campus and the students had spilled out onto the pavement. One particular group of young men was being quite rowdy and a couple of them called out to us as we neared. I was feeling

A Strange Encounter at Little Hubery

rather threatened and urged George to hurry along and to take a different route home to avoid passing them when he stopped and took my arm and led me down a quiet side street. I could hear the young men whistling and jeering and being generally rather crude, and I looked up into George's beautiful kind eyes and then…' She stopped and covered her face.

'You needn't continue dear, if it upsets you,' said Lady Agnes, taking Ellen's hand and gently rubbing it like a mother might to a distressed child. Ellen smiled at her, thankful for the kind gesture.

'George and I became lovers. It all started out innocently enough. We would meet and take tea in Betty's, which was quite the thing. Sometimes we'd go to the Rialto and afterwards he would walk me home. His wife, Madeline, was a sickly woman prone to melancholia. They were a childless couple and I know George was not happy in the marriage. They had been childhood friends and I believe he married her for that reason only. Their families were friends and I suspect he was coerced into doing so.'

She glanced up at Robert, but he refused to meet her eyes. She carried on. A sick feeling in the pit of her stomach worsened as she spoke.

'We loved each other so, we really did. George lamented ever having met his wife but I knew he would never leave her…unless.'

'Unless…' ventured Travers. Ellen sighed miserably and mumbled something incoherent.

'Speak up dear,' said Lady Agnes. Again Ellen began to sob, trying to speak but unable to stop the flow of tears, her whole body wracked with the violence of it.

'Someone do something. Oh please, please stop dear child,' said Lady Agnes, distraught at the spectacle unfolding. Travers took a step forward and took Ellen firmly but gently by the shoulders.

'Ellen, you'll feel much better for getting this off your chest.' Ellen looked at Travers and for the first time saw only kindness and genuine concern in his eyes and in his warm smile.

'Thank you Mr Travers,' she sniffed. 'I believe you're right. When it became clear to me that there were weak spots within the marriage I…I started to look for ways to break it down.'

A Strange Encounter at Little Hubery

Lady Agnes tutted and shook her head.

'I was besotted with him. Madeline's feelings didn't even come into it.' Ellen's tears had dried now and there was a steely determination, an undisguised anger to her voice. The others looked at this new Ellen with a mixture of bewilderment and contempt.

'One day she visited him at the school. I happened to be passing through reception at the time and the school secretary asked me if I knew where Mr Sinclair was as his wife was in reception and she couldn't get hold of him. Well I stood frozen to the spot! I spun around and gave her a good hard look. She was pretty enough I suppose, if you liked that kind of thing, but so pale, so fragile. Well I told the secretary I would see if he was in the library as I was going up that way and was pretty certain he would be. I told her if I wasn't down in a few minutes that it was because Geo…*Mr Sinclair* was indeed there and she should have one of the pupils take her up. I knew he was up there. I knew he'd been marking the students work and was alone. Sure enough, Mrs Sinclair waited and then came up to the library as suggested, and according to plan walked straight in and caught George and I in a steamy clinch. Well she let out a blood-curdling scream and ran as fast as she could from the building. George gave me a look that made my blood run cold and then ran after her. What I hadn't planned on was the pupil, a thirteen-year-old girl, coming into the library with her.'

'The fallout was horrendous,' continued Ellen. 'The pupil was traumatised, George was horrified and I was suspended indefinitely pending an investigation. George, who took leave until the end of term and the New Year, never contacted me again. For months I never left the house. My family were mortified and naturally my job was at stake. It became imperative I leave York. The school offered to give me a glowing reference with regards to my work if I offered to 'move on' I believe was the term used. But there were no openings to be found. I became desperate, and then the unthinkable happened.'

Arthur handed her a glass of brandy and she took it gratefully, wincing as the liquid burned the back of her throat.

A Strange Encounter at Little Hubery

'Madeline, it seems, never recovered from the shock of what she had seen in the library. Her nerves were shot. She became even more withdrawn and was confined to her room. She refused to speak to anyone, especially George, who I believe she never spoke to again however much he begged and pleaded. One afternoon George had to take a trip into town and he promised Madeline he wouldn't be too long. The trip must have taken him longer than he anticipated and when he returned...' She gave a deep sigh, her sorrow plain to see. 'When he returned he found Madeline slumped across the bed, her face and lips blue.'

'Oh!' cried out Lady Agnes.

'No, she wasn't dead,' said Ellen flatly. 'No, she'd taken every pill she could lay her hands on. A concoction of pain killers, anti-depressants, sleeping pills etc., and if George had found her one minute later... They rushed her to hospital comatose and pumped out the contents of her stomach. When she finally awoke she was...how shall I say...a vegetable? Brain damaged beyond repair.'

'Lack of oxygen!' volunteered the professor. 'Poor child...terrible business.'

Ellen paused, the tears streaming down her face. Not sobs. Silent, heartfelt tears. Tears of genuine remorse.

'Yes…terrible. A terrible burden.' She sniffed and wiped the tears from her cheeks. Her eyes were red and puffy and she suddenly looked much older.

'It's hard to believe that was only two weeks ago. The people in town shunned my family. They threw things at the windows and shouted horrible things as they passed. George, it seems, was considered to have suffered enough, and so he had poor fellow, so he had. Then, I received a letter from my Aunt in Redcar who had managed to secure me a position in a school in Northumberland in which she had been headmistress. That is where I'm going now, or was before this dreadful storm.

After a moment of silence Ellen blew her nose and composed herself. 'I hope you will never have cause to feel the remorse I'm feeling right now. I robbed that woman of her marriage and then her life. I will go to my grave with these feelings, and every time I close my eyes, I will always be haunted with images of Madeline

A Strange Encounter at Little Hubery

as she was on that day we first met in the school reception hall.'

The weary travellers sat in subdued silence. The station at Little Hubery stood frozen in time, like a relic from the past. Not even the wind could be heard, nor the ticking of the clock in the old waiting room. In a small store room at the back of the station, a body lay shrouded in a blanket. Nearby, a shadowy figure stood at the kitchen window, his face a pale mask in the dimly lit surrounds. A thin hand felt around the window frame for a niche and found one. The gaunt hand slid open the sash and the figure climbed in…

Ellen had fallen asleep, exhausted by her ordeal. The others, shocked by the revelation, sat in a brooding silence. Robert was becoming increasingly agitated and had drunk a little more than he should have on an empty stomach. Travers was troubling him, although he now seemed more devil's advocate than demon. It still begged the question how the hell he knew so much about the others, complete strangers stranded in the waiting room. Waiting room? What were they waiting for anyway in this eerie place with the telephone lines down and people creeping around the station? Surely now the storm had abated, he and Arthur could walk into town. He approached the stationmaster, who shook his head doubtfully.

'We're a small backwater I'm afraid. Even if we could make it across the sodden moorland, which in itself is extremely doubtful, we'd never be able to get a car back to the others. The roads will be flooded for miles around and who knows what damage the wind has done. The lines are down. I can't even see the signal lights anymore. I've lost contact with the box. Far better we stay within the safe confines of the station than go wandering about before daybreak.'

'Safe confines huh?' Robert gave a small laugh bordering on hysterical. His weariness was evident, but his nerves kept him on edge.

'Why don't you try and get some rest. We'll...' Arthur stopped dead at the look of horror on the soldier's face. Suddenly he heard a cry of fear from Lady Agnes and turned to look behind. Everyone in the room except Ellen, who

A Strange Encounter at Little Hubery

was sleeping, were on their feet and staring with fear and shock towards the dark corner and the door that led into the back rooms of the station.

Chapter Twenty-Four

The solider crept forward and signalled to the station master to stand tight against the wall to the left-hand side of the door. The others watched in horror as the door slowly opened, revealing the darkness beyond. The professor put a protective arm around the old lady who sat mouth agape, paralysed with fear. Everyone held their breath. Travers crept forward from his corner by the fire and watched expressionless as a form materialised slowly from the shadowy corridor. Robert quick as a flash raised his arms and dealt the emerging figure a blow to the shoulder blades and sent him crashing to the floor.

'That's him,' screamed the old lady. 'That's the ghost.'

'Percy?' Arthur cried in astonishment to his recumbent clerk as the man lay moaning on the floor. 'What the bloody hell are you doing creeping round the station at night?' Arthur and

A Strange Encounter at Little Hubery

Robert helped him to his feet and Percy winced, looking warily at the soldier who had dealt him the blow.

Ellen, disturbed by the fracas, sat up rubbing her hazy eyes and stared bemused at the stranger before her.

'Well Percy?' said Arthur, as confused as the rest.

They led Percy to a chair by the fire, and Arthur poured him a brandy. His clothes were wet and he shivered uncontrollably as he gazed at the fire.

'I've been sleeping at the station Arthur,' he volunteered flatly. 'Dorothy and me, we've been having a few problems.' He looked around sheepishly, embarrassed at having to disclose his personal business to strangers, the others equally embarrassed at bearing witness to it.

'You fool,' chided Arthur. 'You know it's against railway company regulations. You could have come and stayed at the house.'

Percy stared morosely into the flames and Arthur wondered how he'd not noticed the change in his normally cheerful clerk. He tapped him on the back.

'All's well now, Percy. I'm sure Dot will come to her senses soon. Until then you can stay with me.'

A Stranger's Tale

Ernest Sykes didn't like him at all, of that he was certain! And the newly appointed manager of the bank ruled with an iron fist. But with an exemplary work record, the soon to be son-in-law of Mayor Sir William Bainbridge knew he was first in line for promotion to Nervous Norman's old position of supervisor. For the first time in ages his future looked rosy. In two weeks' time he would be married. He'd bought his fiancée the ring she desired and booked their honeymoon to Venice. He'd kept a record of monies he had taken from each account and fully intended on his promotion to supervisor to pay them back, gradually of course, plus a little added interest to cover what they would have earned. He wasn't a bad man, not really. It wasn't really fraud was it? Just a loan to tide him over. He'd make good on his promotion. Then he could settle down to married life and his new job at the bank. God willing.

Chapter Twenty-Five

'We thought you were a ghost, Percy,' said Lady Agnes, smiling at the shivering clerk. 'That's clears up that mystery at least.'

'It doesn't explain everything that's happened though, does it?' replied Ellen. 'I mean it explains our intruder, but what about the other things?'

'Other things?' Percy looked up at Arthur, puzzled.

'Radio interference, phone lines down, that kind of thing. What with the storm and the untimely death of Sir Gregory, things have been really creepy down here tonight.'

Percy shuddered 'I saw the, the…I saw him lying in the back office. What?'

'A heart attack, judging by the bluish tinge around his lips,' interjected the professor, smiling at the old lady tenderly. 'Could have happened at any time.'

'And what about the ghost train?' said Ellen. 'You saw it,' she said addressing the stationmaster.

'I saw something, I confess,' said Arthur, made uncomfortable by the scrutiny. 'But my dear, we're all exhausted and under a great deal of stress. We have just witnessed the death of a gentleman and it's not everyday one sees a dead body! Sorry.' He offered his heartfelt apologies to Lady Agnes, as though he'd forgotten she was present.

'I've seen plenty,' said the soldier grimly.

'I've seen more than I could ever want to,' replied the professor sadly. All turned to look to him.

'My old school friend Francis and I were the best of pals since infancy,' the professor began. 'Our parents were friends and we were inseparable for a good many years. Francis was very small for his age and he was a quiet, gentle boy, but I have never in all my days of academia known such intellect, such brilliance, nor anyone with such an extraordinary capacity for learning and storing information.' He smiled to himself, a sad smile of memories faded with time, of innocence lost. The others waited patiently. 'The boy was an undisputed genius and although I strived hard to keep up, I'm afraid I paled in comparison. Truth is, I would not have achieved what I have academically where it not for his help and his patience. But my story I'm afraid is an old one.' A sudden clap of thunder and the sound of the driven rain made Ellen shudder. She looked earnestly at the professor. 'As we grew older, so we grew apart. Not that we weren't still friends, but I got in with a rather rowdy crowd and Francis, hard as he tried, was simply not accepted.' He looked around at the faces of his companions. 'He was introverted you see, not very physical, and the other fellows mocked him. In fact they bullied him over his lack of prowess on the sports field and for his gentle nature, and to my shame in my desperate need to belong, I also belittled and ridiculed my dearest friend.' He sighed. 'Now don't take me wrong, I was no Stanley Engelhart, but I was a mean bowler and wicket-keeper and I could hold my own at football too.'

Arthur broke away from the gathering to make Percy a hot drink and tend to the fire.

'One evening we were all celebrating the end of our exams and had managed to smuggle, with the help of one the older boys, two bottles of cheap scotch into our dormitories.' He paused. 'Not being used to such strong liquor or any liquor at all for that matter, we soon lost control. Francis, who in an aim to prove himself had drunk the most, had become bolder by the minute.' The professor shook his head as the memories came flooding back. 'Suddenly Wareing, one of the head boys, stood and we all followed him outside to the bell tower where the school flag hung. I was terrified. I knew what he would do. He dared Francis to climb the tower and steal the flag. I begged him not to do it, but he pulled away from me and with an amazing fleetness of foot scaled the ivy on the side of the tower.'

The professor sat wringing his hands. Arthur returned with hot drinks and settled by the fire with the others.

'The others cheered him on but I couldn't look. I knew he was trying to impress me and my friends, to prove himself worthy of being one of the boys. I also knew I was partly to blame. He soon reached the parapet and climbed over, and with a sigh of relief I waved to him at the top.'

A Strange Encounter at Little Hubery

'Thank you,' said the professor with a smile, taking a steaming mug from Ellen. He took a sip and the hot liquid singed his lips. He continued.

'He removed the flag as we watched intently, the boys spurring him on, but for reasons known only to himself he removed the pole too, instead of just unclipping the flag. We shouted up to him *no, Francis, no*, but he seemed not to hear us. He was just under half way down when the edge of the flagpole he was carrying under his arm got caught in the ivy. He pulled and twisted but he couldn't get it loose. *No Francis, leave it*, I cried out. The other boys were silent now, sobered, anxiously watching as the foolish boy tried to remove the pole from the ivy that held it entangled.

Suddenly the pole broke free, the impetus unbalancing Francis as he clung desperately to the thickest branch of ivy he could, crying out in his fear for us to save him. I ran forward, but Wareing held me back. *No you fool, the ivy won't hold the both of you*. I struggled but I knew he was right. *Francis*, I cried out in desperation.'

The others drew in closer. Outside the wind began to howl. Reflections of dancing flames licked the ceiling.

'All at once the ivy was pulled away from the wall with the weight of the clinging boy. We all gasped in horror and it seemed as if, just for the briefest spell, time had stood still. Then everything moved, but really slowly as though time was trying to catch up with itself. A strange smile seemed to cross Francis' face and he began to plummet towards the ground. For some reason he turned in mid air before falling. The flag pole had already begun its descent and stuck into the grass at the foot of the tower and then the unthinkable happened. Francis fell face down with incredible force and impaled himself upon the pole sticking upright in the wet grass.' The professor sniffed away a tear, embarrassed by his public display of emotion so long after the fact.

'He never made a noise as he fell but let out a grunt as his body was skewered by the pole. For a second or two we stood rigid with shock, and then we all ran forward towards the now still body of our friend. Wareing retched and then vomited at the sight that greeted us, for the

A Strange Encounter at Little Hubery

weight of Francis' body had caused it to slide full length down the pole, only its tip pinning him to the ground. *Help me*, I cried as I tried to free him. I knew he was dead, of course I did, but I couldn't bear to see him like that.'

Ellen had begun to sob and Lady Agnes put a comforting arm around her shoulders. Percy looked as if he too was about to vomit.

'A couple of the boys ran up, adrenalin playing its part as we removed the pole from his back. We turned him around, and although a trickle of blood escaped from his lips, he looked every bit as peaceful as if he were lying out on the lawns in the sun. His eyes were wide as if in wonder and he smiled peacefully up at us. The boys backed off as if repulsed and closing his lids with my fingers, I rested my head against his blood-soaked shirt and howled in anguish.'

When he was finished the professor hung his head in shame and remorse. Travers placed a comforting hand on one shoulder and smiled at the professor.

'Professor you were not to blame. It was a boyish prank gone wrong. You couldn't have prevented it. It was just one of those things.'

Everyone looked at Travers in shock. What the hell was this man about? Cruelly probing one minute, offering solace the next. The wind groaned like a wounded beast and the gaslights flickered and then went out, only the fire illuminating the scene, casting grotesque shadows on the walls. But none were more so than the silhouette of the stooped man who loomed over the prone and broken figure of the professor.

Chapter Twenty-Six

Arthur watched weary-eyed as the minute hand moved slowly around the clock face. It was a little after four a.m. and the others were sleeping, but exhausted as he was, he could not manage to drop off. Percy and Robert had spread out on the floor in front of the fire, and both ladies were curled up on benches. The professor slumbered where he sat; even Travers appeared to have worn himself out. He thought of Percy sleeping at the station. How could he have not known? He smiled at his clerk snoring peacefully by the fire. Percy was a good lad, and he was sure all would fine soon enough between him and his good lady.

The wireless had been switched off and all was silent but for the ticking of the clock. The thunder and lightning had passed over but the wind still howled around the station building, not with the same ferocity, but enough to drive the pouring rain hard against the waiting room windows.

What a bloody night, he thought to himself, looking round at the stranded passengers sleeping as peacefully as babes. Who would have thought when they first settled together by the fire that they harboured such secrets? The late judge in the back room, an honourable and respected gentleman, guilty of sending an innocent man to his death. The professor plagued with a deep-seated sense of guilt over a tragic and unfortunate accident. And what of the young lady, Ellen, inadvertently ruining the life of another by attempting to steal her husband? What a dark horse she turned out to be. What other secret's would be revealed before the night was out, and what part would the enigmatic Travers have to play in prompting that? Although he knew he himself had led a good, honest life and had no secrets to hide or nothing to fear from Travers, he still felt uneasy in the other man's company. It seemed Travers had been doing his level best to antagonise the soldier, but to what end?

He hoped for no more secret revelations, no more bombshells dropped. There had been

A Strange Encounter at Little Hubery

enough horror stories around the campfire this night.

He felt cramped and achy and stretched out his arms and legs, the damaged knee causing a sharp pain to shoot up his leg. He thought it would be best to try and keep it flexible so it wouldn't seize up, and to this end he decided to walk through and try the phone again, although in truth he held out little hope. Sometimes they were down for days, and it was a good job the signal boxes didn't have to rely on the same line. He thought of radioing down to his signalman. He'd tried a couple of times earlier, but was met with the same static that had interfered with the wireless. He knew young Jack wouldn't have much to tell him, isolated as he was in his signal box, but Arthur knew he should keep trying if only to see how the lad was.

When he approached the door to his office, he felt apprehension, like a knot in his stomach. Not fear exactly but something akin to it. He paused, wondering what was waiting for him behind the door. He knew he had to face whatever it was, but he also knew instinctively that it meant him no harm.

As he entered, the room felt cold; there was also a strange smell, pipe smoke mixed with… he couldn't quite place it, but it was a familiar smell in many ways and one that stirred up long dormant memories of childhood. He made his way over to the radio and tried calling out, but the terrible static told him he'd have no joy with the instrument. He turned and was just about to try the telephone again when a figure sat in his chair surprised him, and he let out a startled cry.

'D-dad?' he gasped. His father's shade wavered and fluctuated, now translucent, now solid. The very air around him seemed to quiver as though he had upset the natural balance of things by appearing now to his son. His clothes were colourless and grey as though washed many, many times, and his eyes seemed hollow yet somehow flat, without dimension.

Suddenly, Arthur felt the room spinning. He felt light-headed and had to lean against the wall to stop himself from falling. A mist descended and when his vision had cleared, he found himself not in his own office, but in the same room as it had been when it was his father's office all those years ago. His father's old mining lamp stood on the desk beside the

A Strange Encounter at Little Hubery

Marconi and his favourite fountain pen and blotter shared a space with an inkpot and some rolled up sheets. The pigeonholes on his desk were overflowing with documents and his barometer held pride of place on the wall. The old clock was the same, but for a second it appeared to be going backwards, and then it stopped.

Arthur caught sight of an old picture of his mother and himself when he was but a boy. He was wrapped in a towel and she was rubbing him and hugging him at the same time. He gave out a small cry.

'I remember when this was taken. I was seven and we went to Whitby. My dad had just been teaching me to fly a kite on the beach, and I chased it into the sea and got soaked.' He felt tears welling up in his eyes and then his father walked in.

'Cup of tea, Albert?' Arthur heard from beyond the open door. It was Walter, Dad's former clerk before he himself took over after returning from the Somme. Albert and Walter alive again, in the flesh. Arthur rushed over to his father, but he seemed not to notice him and brushed straight past and sat down at his desk.

Jack C. Phillips

Arthur felt hurt by the rebuff and turned to look at his father who was busy with the wireless. He left the office and walked through the booking hall to the waiting room. He could hear Walter in the tiny back room that served as the station's kitchen, whistling 'Underneath the Mellow Moon,' and when he walked through to the waiting room, he gasped in surprise. The others were gone and it was daylight, a bright sunny day. The waiting room was full of passengers wearing the clothes of days gone by. Suddenly, a lady wearing a cloche hat and dressed in a jersey blouse and a velour skirt walked straight through him as though he wasn't there. He saw her shudder and felt a jolt of electricity through his entire body. For a second there they had almost become one. He could feel what she was feeling, could see her thoughts. She was meeting her fiancé and they were to look at rings. She was excited, full of joy and expectation, this lady…Elizabeth. Her name was Elizabeth. The lady turned and he smiled at her, but she seemed to look straight through him.

A voice behind him made him jump. It was Travers.

A Strange Encounter at Little Hubery

'They cannot see us Arthur,' he said, smiling warmly at the stationmaster. 'We're just ghosts in their time.'

'Travers? What is this? Where are we?'

'Why, Arthur,' Travers teased, not unkindly. 'Little Hubery. Do you not recognise your own station?'

'Scarcely,' said Arthur. 'But how and where are my passengers? I left them sleeping.'

'They're still there.' Travers smiled. 'They have not moved.' Arthur looked at Travers as if he'd gone mad. Could he see something Arthur couldn't?

'They're where you left them Arthur, in nineteen thirty-six. This is nineteen twenty-three.' He gestured with a sweep of his arm at the room around him. Arthur looked at him with open-mouthed astonishment.

'It's a time-slip Arthur. A rare phenomenon indeed. You are very lucky to have witnessed this.'

'But how Travers? And why only you and I? Why not the others?'

Travers sighed. 'The others are sleeping. Only you and I were awake when the phenomenon occurred, so only you and I must witness it.'

Arthur looked around him and reached out to touch the wall. It was solid, it was real. He suddenly became suspicious of Travers and wondered what game he was playing now.

'What is this Travers? How do you know these things? What are you doing here and why was that lady able to shift through me when the walls feel so solid?'

Travers sighed again, growing impatient. 'The walls are solid Arthur. The station hasn't changed. It's still all around us. Only the timeframe has changed. We are visitors in another time. We are inconsequential. We have no solid form, we're just voyeurs. Spectators in an era past.'

'So none of this is real?' said Arthur.

'Of course it's real, man. It's a real as you or I.'

Suddenly Arthur began to feel anxious, to feel wrong, displaced. He noticed that the lighting had changed and that the people around him seemed to be wavering, solid one minute, ethereal the next. He looked back at Travers and although he could see the other man's lips

A Strange Encounter at Little Hubery

moving, he couldn't really work out what Travers was trying to say. His words were slurred and seemed muffled, as though he was in another room. Arthur's unease grew as his surroundings became flat and everything turned still around him. Not even the air moved.

'Travers!' he tried to say but found himself unable to form the words. Arthur turned and walked back through the ticket office. He found he could no longer hear Walter whistling or his father talking or moving around. Everything was deathly silent.

The ground seemed to shift beneath his feet and he again found himself grabbing the door frame for support. Everything went black for a second, and then he found himself staring at his office door. He reached for the handle and pushed. Within, the room had returned to normal. On his desk he could see the telephone and his typewriter, the small table under the window where the wireless normally stood. The fire burned low in the grate and beside it, in his father's old armchair sat Travers.

Chapter Twenty-Seven

'My father, Albert, took me on as an apprentice when I was fourteen,' said Arthur, passing a drink to Travers. 'I'd grown up around the railway. Before he took over at Little Hubery, he was stationmaster at Shearing's Vale and Doncaster before that, where I was born in the station house.' He pulled up a chair by the fire and sipped his scotch. He felt the need of a stiffener after his recent experience.

'At fourteen I became apprentice fireman before showing an aptitude as a signal man, the position I took at Shearing's Vale before being drafted into the army.' Half of Travers' face was lit by the glow of the newly refreshed fire, and Arthur couldn't help but notice how smooth his face now looked. He hadn't realised Travers was so young. He didn't look a day over twenty-five. Even the events of the previous night didn't seem to have had an effect on him. No

A Strange Encounter at Little Hubery

shadows showed beneath his eyes, which were clear and bright. He looked for all intents and purposes refreshed, like a man who had just had his eight hours. Arthur again brushed off the feelings of unease he had come to feel when Travers was around and continued.

'When he was moved to Little Hubery following the death of its current stationmaster, I stayed on as signal man at the Vale for a couple of years before moving to the box at Hubery. I found the isolation of being on signal played with my nerves, and when Walter retired in the autumn of twenty–three, I moved to the ticket office there and began to work closely with Dad, who was training me to step into his position when he retired. He was a hard taskmaster and showed me no favours for being his son, but I knew that stepping into his shoes as stationmaster would be no easy challenge, and I worked all the harder to please him.

'Only a few months after I'd moved to Hubery, we lost Mum to pneumonia. Dad was never the same after that and his health seriously declined. The company had offered him early retirement with full pension after all his years of service, but he held on until he had full confidence in my ability to take over at the helm. Finally in the spring of twenty-five, I was made stationmaster at Little Hubery. For a while things ran smoothly. Dad was exhausted and spent many of his waking hours by the sea, claiming the fresh salt air was beneficial to his health. But he was a working man, had been since as far back as he could remember, and he was soon bored with the inertia of his days and back at the station, making his presence felt.'

He drained his glass and fell silent for a moment, staring into the flames. Travers watched him patiently, waiting for him to continue with the story.

'As an old-school stationmaster, Dad was always resistant of change, and when he retired the railway company decided to introduce more modern equipment and methods of working. But Dad wasn't about to make for an easy transition and nothing could persuade him that his interference wasn't welcome. I should really have foreseen that he would have problems letting go, especially without Mum to fill his days. As the weeks and months passed, he had more or less moved back in at the station and his reluctance to retire was causing me all manner of problems.' Arthur sighed. 'He would undermine me with the workers and over-ride any decisions I would make with regards to staffing and the running of the station. When, one day, he had almost caused an accident by interfering with the signal box and not allowing for the passing on of a message from Clarings Brook about allowing a goods train into our section, I had to ban him from the station by orders of the company. This put further strain on our relationship, and as we also shared a home, things became very difficult between us. We spent most of our evenings bickering and arguing. Dad was a shadow of his former self, and it's always hard to watch a beloved parent go that way, but more so when he refused to let go. Nothing I could say could persuade him to go out, meet his friends and enjoy his retirement years.'

Arthur suddenly became morose and Travers smiled kindly and prompted him to go on.

'On that particular afternoon, we'd spent most of the previous evening arguing about the suitability of a new signalman the company had hired and I was tired of it, and if the truth be known, tired of him too.' He hung his head in shame.

'When I left for work that morning, he had begged me to let him go too, claiming he was feeling unwell and just wanted to sit in the office by the fire. He promised not to interfere, but I was adamant that he stay up at the house, especially if he was, as he claimed, unwell. He had used that line several times before so I would allow him into the office, whereupon he had made a miraculous recovery and taken over the running of the station. At one prompt, I had left the office and gone up to the house to make Dad a sandwich and found him slumped in his chair, staring sightlessly out of the window at the comings and goings of the station. He was dead!'

Arthur sighed. His distress and his feelings of guilt were apparent.

'If only I'd let him come with me. I didn't believe he was ill. I was angry and resentful and I didn't get to say goodbye. He'll never know how much I love him.'

Travers stood and walked towards the door, stopping behind Arthur's chair and placing a reassuring arm on his shoulder.

A Strange Encounter at Little Hubery

'Arthur, you have nothing to reproach yourself for. You were as good a son as any man could hope for. Your father has no ill feelings towards you. He loves you and wants you to be happy. He wants you to let these feelings go Arthur. Leave them be and move on.' Arthur heard Travers' voice emulating that of his father and echoing around the room, and just for the briefest amount of time, he saw him again, smiling from his chair by the fire. He heard the door click gently behind him, but he didn't look round, didn't move for what seemed like an age. He simply sat in his office chair, staring into the flames as the darkness from the moor crept ever closer to the isolated station and its six stranded inhabitants.

A Stranger's Tale

The sun beat down mercilessly, the heat intensified by the huge plate glass window opposite his desk. He ran his finger around the inside of his collar in a desperate bid to loosen it and cool himself down a little. If only he could remove his jacket! But he knew that would be frowned upon by his new manager, Sykes. The clerks and tellers were cool in cotton shirts and ties, but as newly appointed supervisor, he was expected to set an example. It was fine for the bank manager and assistant bank manager to remove their jackets in the comfort of their own offices, their own *fan-cooled* offices, but he, as banking hall supervisor was customer-facing so no such concession was made for him.

He shifted awkwardly in his seat. His flesh, only an hour or so since lightly cologned and fresh, felt prickly and sticky, and his back was drenched with perspiration. His discomfort was

A Strange Encounter at Little Hubery

further heightened by a fresh attack of nerves at the thought of his impending nuptials only two days from now and of his ever swelling bank account, or rather that of his alias Basil Morgan-Jones. He groaned as Mrs Baxter entered the banking hall and made a beeline for his desk.

Chapter Twenty-Eight

Robert wasn't sure what had awakened him so abruptly and he looked around bleary-eyed for a moment or two before focussing on the chimney corner. Travers wasn't there, but some movement had caught his eye and he stared disbelievingly at what he saw.

A shadow, nebulous and vague, seemed to cover the wall in the very corner, like a mould, and it seemed to be moving, growing one minute, retreating the next. It was black like an ink stain, impenetrable in parts, and these parts too seemed to be moving, thinning out, breaking apart before forming in other areas. In the more opaque parts of the melee, he could just make out shapes forming.

He looked around to see if any of the others were awake, but they all seemed dead to the world. Arthur was in his office and Travers was strangely absent. He turned back to the alcove.

A Strange Encounter at Little Hubery

The shadow seemed to have spread, to be moving down the wall. He felt his chest tighten and his hands felt clammy, his breathing laboured. He tried to move away from the thing in the corner, but he found himself frozen to the spot. He could hear the gentle snores of the professor. The old lady and the girl also seemed to be sleeping peacefully, as though in telling their stories to the others they had somehow unburdened themselves.

A strange groaning sound filled the room and seemed to be getting louder, and still the others never stirred. Robert was unsure whether it was the wind in the chimney breast or whether it came from the abomination in the room. Whatever it was, it was his to witness and his alone, for although he tried to cry out, his fears could not find a voice. His windpipe felt restricted, his mouth dry and his tongue unable to detach itself from his lower jaw.

The swirling, black mass seemed to move away from the corner and on to the chimney breast itself, coming to rest on the wall and hovering above the mantle. Unlike before, the room remained warm, the gaslights unwavering, and the fire burned evenly and brightly. Nothing was untoward in the room but for the moving shadow above the fireplace, from which exuded such feelings of hatred and evil towards Robert that he was sure he would die from terror right where he sat, on the floor in front of the fireplace.

From out of the black mist, a hand formed and reached out towards Robert and then another, both vaporising before reaching him. The centre of the mass seemed to converge and a shape began to form, a torso, but vague and insubstantial, malformed and without a core. Robert thought his heart would stop when a head formed above the torso, the features ill-defined and tenuous, but features he recognised nonetheless. It was the man whose murder he had witnessed and not attempted to prevent. A man who would haunt and plague him for the rest of his life unless justice for his untimely and violent death was seen to be done. The head groaned its injustice and twisted this way and that as if in immense pain. Then it fixed its shadowy, black pits of eyes on its antagonist and a desolate cry rent the still night air.

A Strange Encounter at Little Hubery

Robert passed out when it extended a long, snake-like neck and rushed screaming towards him.

Chapter Twenty-Nine

'Robert? Robert, wake up.' He felt himself being shaken roughly by the shoulder. 'Robert, wake up. You're having a bad dream.'

Robert opened his eyes wide and looked around him at the alarmed faces of the other passengers. Travers had a hand on his arm, and Robert jumped back as if it were contagious. He looked toward the shadowy alcove and up at the chimney breast, but there was nothing. The others stared at him as if he were mad, their expressions a mixture of bemusement and concern. Arthur came running in from his office, and Travers gestured for him to stand back.

'Are you quite well dear fellow?' remarked the professor. 'You were screaming, old man. Gave us quite a fright.' Travers extended his hand to help the soldier up, but he knocked it away aggressively.

A Strange Encounter at Little Hubery

'Come,' said Travers. 'You'll feel much better when you've unburdened yourself. Why don't you tell us all about it?'

'You!' the soldier screamed, lunging at him. 'You did this you, you monster. What the hell are you that you know the inside of another's mind?' Arthur, Percy and the professor rushed Robert, who fought them fiercely. Soon they overpowered him and pinned him back into a chair. The ladies fled and stood by the ticket office counter, upset by the latest disturbance. Travers held his ground.

Eventually Robert calmed down and stared long and hard into the fire. The others turned to move away, troubled by his demeanour but not wanting to bother him further, but the soldier called them back. He sighed and for a minute or two his head fell upon his chest, but then he raised it again and looked them all in the eye, and his look was grave and deadly serious.

'It's true,' he said sadly, 'I too have a tale to tell. I served with the British Army in India for three years in the Eastern Command, based in Lucknow North East India. I myself was stationed at a camp in Bengal. Our platoon consisted of four sections. Near the camp was a small village, Adra, next the town of Haora, where we would go for supplies. Some of the lads had women in the town, but one of our platoon would sneak off to the village instead. He showed no interest in the women in town and we wondered if he was…you know?' He looked up at the ladies, embarrassed. He cleared his throat and carried on. 'He had no wife at home and kept pretty much to himself, out of the way. A queer sort he was.' Robert rubbed his eyes as though suddenly weary.

'A few times we caught him creeping off and wondered where he went and what he was up to, so one night we followed him. It was just getting dark and some of the village's children were still playing in the street. He approached them and offered them chocolate. A couple of them ran away, but he stood talking to the others and then led one of them away out of the village. We tried to follow him, but he seemed to know the area quite well and disappeared into some trees with the child, a girl aged around nine. Some of the men waited for him. They wanted to kill him then and there. Many of us had children, daughters, and I could understand their frustration, their rage, but I wanted him

A Strange Encounter at Little Hubery

punished through official channels. If he was found guilty, he would be put to death anyway. The outcome would be the same, but we wouldn't have blood on our hands.

'The next day men came from the village for help. The girl was missing. We scoured the area but could find no trace of her. Then someone spotted him, Powell was his name, William Powell, with scratches down his face. He ran away with four of our men plus a couple from the village in pursuit. I stayed behind to help with the search. Suddenly I heard a gut-wrenching cry of anguish, a heart-rending scream. I hear it even now, as clear as if it were yesterday. The girl's father stepped out from the trees; he had something in his hands, something limp like a bundle of rags. He dropped to his knees and threw his head back and wailed. I was consumed with pity for the man and horror at what had taken place. But my heart was truly broken when the girl's mother appeared. She coolly and silently walked over to her husband, removed a strand of hair from her daughter's eyes and took her indoors. Just as calmly as if she'd been sleeping and she was putting her to bed. The girl's neck lolled at an un-natural angle, and it was obvious it had been broken.

'Back at camp we searched his cabinet in his bunker and found, erm, souvenirs, among them a girl's slipper, a cheap tin bracelet and some dead flowers. The men were furious. Some cried, either with rage or because they were fathers away from their own children. A search party was set up, the others having lost Powell when he jumped on a passing lorry heading into town.

'We split up into two groups and then we split again within our group. I was partnered with a young subaltern named Harris, and for a while we managed to stay together in the bustling streets of the town. Then suddenly I found myself having to jump out of the path of an approaching rickshaw, and when I turned back to find Harris, he was gone. I wandered the streets for ages looking for members of my platoon. It was baking hot and dusty, and I looked around for somewhere to buy a drink and then I heard a ruckus in a nearby alleyway.

'Four of the platoon had Powell up against a wall and were repeatedly punching him.

A Strange Encounter at Little Hubery

'I stood back and watched. The men hadn't seen me at that point but Powell had. He pleaded with me to help, but I watched and waited. It was my intention to see him beaten for what he had done; it was all I could do not to join in. I meant to stop it, to let justice take its due course, but I didn't. I just kept thinking of the children playing in the village street. Of the little girl taking chocolate and being led off into the woods and how we'd failed to protect her. Of her limp body, so small, so frail. Of her father's anguish and her mother's silent tears, and I took solace from every punch and every kick that bastard took…Sorry! I wanted him to die, slowly, fearful and in pain as he had caused the death of that poor child, so I stood and I watched. Nobody interfered, the people in the street too afraid. I watched as he was slowly beaten to death and all the while he watched me, watching. After a while he stopped begging for help and just watched me with a kind of dull bemusement as if to say, *they're killing me. They're killing me and you're just going to watch.* Eventually his body went limp, but still his eyes watched, dull and lifeless like a fish on a slab, not bemused anymore, but accusing.

Taunting me with what I had witnessed. The men turned when they realised he was dead, and one caught a glimpse of me as they left. A look of understanding passed between us, no words needed.

'The men didn't run, nor did they look back. No-one followed them or tried to challenge them about what had just happened. I too turned away and began walking in the direction I had just come from, and in a while I saw Harris, looking lost among the street traders and the beggars in the baking sun. *Any joy?* he shouted, waving at me. I shook my head and led him away for a drink before we headed back to camp.

'Naturally it wasn't too long before Powell's body was found. Even in that short space of time, the rats and flies had had their fill of him in that dank and dirty alleyway, and it was nothing less than he deserved.

'There was an enquiry into his death of course. Foul play couldn't be ruled out. By this time I had been called back to England, my squadron stationed at Catterick Camp. Back in India the military had been questioning the men about the incident and one had caved in,

A Strange Encounter at Little Hubery

apparently unable to live with himself after the deed. Naturally he didn't implicate any other man, but it was well known by those at camp which men had gone to town to look for Powell in the wake of the little girl's death, and the suspects were soon rounded up. I was lucky not to be implicated myself, only the young subaltern, Harris' testimony that we had spilt from the men and not seen them again until we returned to camp saving me from suspicion. But having been placed in town, I have been called as a witness and must testify before a board of inquiry at Catterick. If I tell the truth of what I witnessed, four good men will die.'

'And if you lie, a man's murder will go unpunished,' said the professor.

'And what of it,' said the soldier. 'He deserved to die for what he did to those children.'

'Who are you to say what man should live and who should die?' Travers spoke out. 'The law decrees he be given a fair trial, and if, as you say, the evidence against him was irrefutable, then he would be put to death anyway. It's not for those men or you to take justice into your own hands.'

The soldier buried his head in his hands and groaned.

'What do I do? What do I do? And now the spirit of Powell haunts me. Out there on the moor, here in the station, where before he only haunted my dreams.'

'Only you can decide what's right, Robert,' said the old lady kindly.

'There is only one proper course of action,' said the professor. 'It's up to you whether you take it or condone a lawless society and a breakdown of justice. If one of the men has already confessed, I see little option open to you other than to speak the truth and let justice prevail.' The others moved away from the soldier, who sat staring into the flames for a good while. Ellen went out to make tea and the old lady followed her. The wind continued to howl and the rain still pounded the windows. Thin streaks of light broke through the heavy storm clouds, driving back the night, and silence pressed heavily against the walls of the station. Finally the soldier stood and looked at the others.

'I have made my decision,' he announced. 'I know what I have to do.'

A Stranger's Tale

Until coming face to face with the old lady, Mrs Baxter, he had cleverly covered his tracks concerning his fraudulent deception and the transferring of monies into his alias' account. Faced with his client's concern about discrepancies in her account, a client of whom he was equally as fond as she was of him, he had led her into his managers' office and there had broken down and confessed all.

He had been instantly suspended pending a full and thorough investigation, only the power and influence of his father-in-law to be, as well as a promise to reimburse all including any interest lost, keeping him from arrest.

'I only wanted the best for Elizabeth.' He sobbed as his fiancée's father led him away, too shame-faced to look his colleagues in the eye. His shame and misery intensified as he heard the old lady wail, 'I would have given him the money if he'd only asked.' Outside, the mayor of Scarborough had warned him to leave and never return. He was never to see his daughter again or look to communicate with her.

Thoroughly wretched and dejected, he'd walked out of town and made for the cool dim shelter of the nearby woodland. There he had sobbed non-stop for the best part of an hour beneath the twisted oak. Finally he stood, brushing himself down and straightening his tie before beginning the ten minute walk down the beaten path to the railway line and bridge three-sixty-one.

He leant against the parapet and straightened his tie. The view from bridge three-sixty-one allowed him to see for miles around, but the woodland, coastline and untamed natural beauty of the surrounding moorland held no charm for him. Not today.

It had been another hot day and the sun was setting on the horizon weaving braids of fiery red across the sky. The man wiped beads of perspiration from his forehead and looked at his fob-watch, only another ten minutes to go and then it would all be over.

A Strange Encounter at Little Hubery

He thought of his fiancée and how he'd let her down. He hoped that she'd understand and that one day she'd be able to forgive him…

Chapter Thirty

In his office Arthur had at last made contact with Shearing's Vale and had learned that the tree had finally been shifted, the line cleared and the points and signalling equipment repaired. In the waiting room his passengers slept unaware that their trial was almost over and they would soon be able to go home. He looked at the clock above the mantle. It was almost five. The numbers swam before him, his head suddenly felt too heavy for his shoulders and all at once, slumped across his desk, the stationmaster slept too.

Travers, deathly still and silent in the chimney corner, rose and stood beside his fellow passengers, watching the sleeping forms in their repose. Soon each would leave the station and go forward with their lives. Some to the same life, others with very different plans, but each man and woman would awake and leave the station changed by his or her experiences the previous night, and Travers could be certain that change was for the better.

He smiled to himself as he watched Lady Agnes, her mouth twitching at the corners as she slept. He knew her new life without her husband would take some adjusting to, but he also knew that she was finally free, of living in his shadow and of his burden of guilt. From across the waiting room he saw the shade of Michael Turner. The boy smiled at him and then turned and walked through the door, disappearing into the darkness of the corridor. Travers looked once more at Lady Agnes who was smiling as she slept, and he knew beyond doubt that her dreams were at last peaceful.

He sat beside the lovely Ellen, asleep on a bench. Her dreams too were of a rosy future now she had finally admitted to her part in the destruction of Madeline Sinclair's mind. Admitted and more importantly regretted and felt genuine pain and remorse for causing damage to her rival in love. Across the miles Madeline Sinclair also slept peacefully. She no longer hurt, nor even remembered her husband's indiscretion. The feelings of hatred and vengeance had only been a result of Ellen's repressed guilt. Ellen would always feel sorry for the pain she had caused George's wife and the damage their affair resulted in, but she knew she had to get on with her life, a good, honest, decent life where recompense would be paid by kind deeds and thoughtful gestures.

From where he sat, Travers could hear the soldier mumbling in his sleep, but he wasn't in the grip of some disturbing nightmare. He was conversing with the man he had wronged and allowed to die, William Powell. Robert was begging forgiveness from the murdered man and vowing to bear witness at the inquiry and see justice done. Travers knew he was salving his conscience and that the trial and prosecution of the murderers would see an end to his nightmares and peace return to the soldier's life at last.

Also in the land of dreams, the professor played cowboys and Indians with Francis, his childhood friend. Francis alive, young again and happy. He told Victor he bore him no ill will. It was after all an accident, a boyish prank gone horribly wrong and that Victor should stop living with the guilt of it and enjoy the time he had left. He assured Victor that one day they

A Strange Encounter at Little Hubery

would meet again, before shooting him dead with an arrow from his bow. The two boys squealed as they ran across the empty field, and a tear ran the length of the professor's cheek before nestling at the end of his nose. Travers laughed as the professor rubbed at the itch before returning to the halcyon sanctum of his dream.

In his office, Arthur dreamed of his parents, his mother laughing as her headscarf was almost blown off in the wind, his dad tanned and happy. They held hands as they walked along the Whitby front, sharing dreams, planning for their future. He sat on a bench and watched them as they passed, oblivious to his presence. 'I'm sorry I wasn't there for you Dad, at the end,' Arthur called out. His dad stopped and turned, a look of bemusement on his face. 'What is it love?' asked Arthur's mother. 'Why, I could have sworn I…' Albert's sentence trailed off and suddenly his eyes met Arthur's and he smiled, lighting up his whole face.

'Arthur,' he said. Now it was his wife's turn to look puzzled.

'Arthur?' she said. Albert McLaren placed his hand lightly on his wife's slightly swollen belly and sighed contentedly.

'The boy's name is Arthur.'

Dawn crept across the storm-tossed moor, the darkness retreating in its wake. It chased away the gloom and banished the angry rolling clouds far across the heath and out to sea. When it reached the station, it pressed against the glass, peering at the prone inhabitants before finding its way inside through gaps in the ill-fitting sashes. It embraced the sleeping passengers, its wispy tendrils like ghostly fingers tracing a path lightly upon their skin, chasing away the shadows and seeing them flee to the sanctuary of the corners.

Travers witnessed the coming of dawn, wearily and not without welcome. He walked across the room, his footsteps barely audible on the parquet, and flung open the waiting room door, stepping out onto the platform and breathing in the fresh salty air. The sky was streaked with red, the occasional cloud hanging like shredded fabric, sheer, ethereal, weightless,

A Strange Encounter at Little Hubery

the last clinging vestiges of the storm waiting to join their indefinable sisters across the water.

The station platform lay defeated about him, the tempest having done its worst, benches tossed aside, detritus blown onto the line, flower-pots smashed and smaller trees uprooted. Signs were torn from their hoardings and lay to rest, mangled at his feet. He kicked aside a twisted advertisement for a local stockist of perambulators on Hubery High Street and made his way towards the end of the platform and down onto the track, whistling as he went. Travers felt peaceful at last. His work was done, his wings earned. In showing others the error of their ways, in hopefully setting them upon the right path, he had atoned for his sin. The sin of taking a life, his own life, James C. Travers, killed August fifth, nineteen-twenty-eight when jumping into the path of an on-coming train from bridge three-sixty-one.

Travers walked awhile along the track, eventually disappearing into the fine mist at first light. Soon all that could be heard was a thin tuneless whistle, until that too was caught up on the gentle morning breeze and swept out to sea.

Epilogue

Lady Agnes Barnes nee Wallace stepped out of the car and walked heavily across the drive and up the steps that lead to the entrance of Beechings, the country house she shared, *had* shared with her spouse, the eminent Sir Gregory Barnes KC. The corners of her mouth upturned slightly at the thought of her late husband. Eminent indeed Gregory, she scoffed lightly at the thought. The weariness and the effects of the previous night's traumatic events seemed to have hit her all at once, and she leaned heavily on the arm of her housekeeper's husband for support. She knew the pain of Gregory's death and the grief at his loss were yet to come, because for all his faults, and there had been many, he was still her husband, the father of her son and she had loved him once. Her housekeeper Mrs Allen smiled kindly at the Lady Agnes, usually so well coiffured but who suddenly looked so old and

A Strange Encounter at Little Hubery

vulnerable. She took the lady's arm, leading her to the first floor bedroom she had shared with her husband.

'I have warmed the sheets for you Lady Agnes,' Mrs Allen said gently as she lowered the old lady onto the bed.

Lady Agnes was asleep before her head hit the pillow. 'Goodnight Gregory,' she murmured before slipping into the safe confines of slumber's warm embrace.

Ellen Potter looked up nervously at the ivy-clad buildings of the school that were to be her new home. She had made it finally and was to report to the headmistress, a Miss Naylor, on arrival. She stepped back on the gravel pathway, avoiding the well-kept lawns now over-shadowed by the ancient school buildings. It was quite dark now and the very tops of the chimneys were shrouded in mist. She thought of the night she and the others had been forced to spend in the waiting room at Little Hubery station, of confessions made, of realisations reached, of epiphanies and fresh starts after the horrors they had been forced to endure. She thought of the others and hoped that they too had profited somehow from their strange encounter that evening. The newly-widowed Lady Agnes, the soldier Robert, his haunting admission and what he had still to face at the trial, and of course the mysterious Travers, whom they had awoken to find missing. Travers with his amazing second sight and the ability to take each and every one of them to a point where they had to confess to their dark secrets, and in doing so had faced their demons and were then able to go forwards with their lives. Who could have guessed they had all hidden such skeletons? Such an innocuous looking group of strangers.

She suddenly felt as though she were being watched and looked to see a small, pale face observing her from an upstairs room Ellen presumed to be a dormitory. She smiled and waved to the little girl who sank back into the shadows, undoubtedly afraid of being chided for being up so late. From somewhere hidden amongst the ivy, she heard a door open and a shaft of light lit up the gravel path, stretching out to the grass beyond before being swallowed by the darkness.

A Strange Encounter at Little Hubery

'Miss Potter? Is that you? Good heavens, such weather we've been having. Well come in dear, come in…' A thin, hawkish-looking woman in a stiff tweed skirt stepped out on to the pathway to shepherd the young teacher indoors. Ellen took once last glance up at the dormitory window, but the little girl had gone.

Dorothy looked anxiously from the window of the little cottage she and husband Percy had shared these past seven years. She had paced the room for most of the night following a nightmare of her husband alone in a room full of evil spirits, wondering if tonight he would return home, if he was safe, where he would find shelter during the storm. She was furious with him for causing her such worry, for his pig-headedness and for the blind jealousies that were threatening to end an othcrwise happy marriage. So what if she wanted a little time away, a hobby, something to broaden her horizons? It was only natural wasn't it? She felt the anger flare up again, like a heat radiating from within. She turned to pace the room and caught sight of their wedding photograph on top of the mantle.

'Oh Percy,' she cried out loud, 'where are you?'

She was startled by a sudden noise outside on the path and she ran to the window to see a rather dishevelled, shame-faced Percy walking up the path. He barely had time to look up before his wife threw open the door and fell sobbing into his arms.

Robert stood facing the board of inquiry. The day he had been dreading had finally arrived. He gave his name, rank and number to the board and with moist palms and a steely resolve, he began to relay his version of events. He told of how Powell had been spotted taking the child into the woods and subsequently followed, but how they had quickly become lost in the thick of the trees. Of how the girl had been reported missing and her body found by villagers after a thorough search of the woodland. He told of how an inspection of the missing Private's things had uncovered items later identified by

A Strange Encounter at Little Hubery

the parents of the village's children as belonging to them.

Robert reported how a group of angry fathers from the platoon and the village had spotted Powell and chased him and how Powell had escaped to Haora on the back of a wagon. Following him to town, they had split into smaller groups, and how in losing his partner he had continued to search alone and that was when he had witnessed the beating that had led to Powell's death. He confessed to his shame in having done nothing to either prevent the attack or to help the victim afterwards. His words were heartfelt and his head hung low as he confessed. He admitted it wasn't his intention to see justice served in that way and nothing on earth could have persuaded him to join in the lynching, but he was moved to tears as he told of the men's anguish at witnessing the pain on the faces of the little girl's parents and the horror they all felt in seeing the limp and lifeless body carried from the woods.

Robert realised he faced a dishonourable discharge from the army and potential imprisonment as an accomplice to the murder, but he felt it was his duty to report what he had witnessed. There could be no doubts in his mind as to Powell's involvement in the little girl's murder, nor that of his platoon mates' involvement in Powell's own, although he pointed out their exemplary records as serving officers of the British army, as well as being fine upstanding civilians. The relief Robert felt as he left the inquest was palpable. Afterwards, before being reunited with his own wife and daughter, he sat alone quietly, his thoughts only for the poor child and her parents.

An investigation into William Powell's past revealed him to be a very unsavoury character indeed, one with several run-ins with the law, although he had never been charged. It also told of his having no surviving relatives. The board brought a verdict of 'death by misadventure,' deciding to deal with the punishment of their men as they saw fit. Robert himself was stripped of his rank, but continued for the time being to be stationed at Catterick Camp training rookies. He was never again bothered by the shade of William Powell, as he had fulfilled his pledge and borne witness to his murder at the trial. Besides if what Robert believed was true,

A Strange Encounter at Little Hubery

Powell faced a much harsher judgement himself, in the afterlife.

Professor Rose kicked at the shingle beneath his feet as his dog snouted amongst the seaweed washed up by the early morning tide. Overhead a curlew cried out, its lonely haunting call rending the still air and setting the professor's nerves on edge.

He sat awhile on a breaker and removed an envelope from his pocket. It was a letter from Lady Agnes, inviting him to pay her a visit in London. He fingered the edge of the paper until it became creased and tattered. He would write back to her at once, accepting her kind invitation, naturally he would. Or maybe he'd leave it, just for a day, or two.

He thought, as he often did, of that night spent in that lonely station waiting room on that storm-tossed moor. Of the people he'd been stranded with, of the secrets they had revealed, and he wondered at their lives going forward. Of the soldier and his trial, of the stationmaster and Percy who were as far as he knew, for he was never to return to Little Hubery, still working there. Of the girl, Ellen and her new job, and of course of Lady Agnes and life without her husband of many years. And then he thought of the man Travers and how he had turned around everyone's lives, pushing them until their fraught nerves could stand no more, forcing the confessions and the epiphanies that inevitably followed, prompting them for the most part to make a clean breast of things, to forgive and to move on with their lives unburdened... free.

Scout, his dog, barked at a crab that had run for cover beneath a large pebble. He pawed at the stone, but it was too embedded, too heavy to dislodge. He soon lost interest in the creature and began attacking a piece of driftwood, taking it between his paws and chewing on it as if it were a juicy bone. The professor turned away and looked out to sea, letting his mind wander again, thinking as he often did of Travers and how unbeknown to the man he had followed him out onto the platform. Even after all he had witnessed that night, how he had watched dumbfounded as the man...as the spirit of the man with whom he had spent the last few hours,

A Strange Encounter at Little Hubery

had walked along the line and disappeared without a trace into the early morning mist.

As the professor slowly rose from his perch, his bones protesting with the effort, he suddenly felt a calmness, a feeling of well-being come over him. Turning to summon his dog, he began his steady walk home. As he walked he fancied he could hear, as he had many times since the night at Little Hubery station, the sound of a man whistling, distant and hollow above the gentle lapping of the waves.

Arthur McLaren, stationmaster at Little Hubery since nineteen twenty-five, smiled up at the clock on his office wall as the nine-fifty-five to Redcar left the station with not a second to spare.

'Regular as clockwork,' he said to no-one in particular as he rose to make a well-earned cup of tea. 'Drink, Colin?' he said to the young lad working the ticket office, Percy's replacement since the lad had been promoted and moved on to Waverley, a main line station up north. Colin nodded in thanks.

Arthur chuckled to himself as he watched two children, a girl and a boy, giggling while they played chase on the platform outside. He knew they were no more than shadows, waifs, a mere echo of what once were, but he didn't mind. He saw them often since that night when he had met James Travers. Them and others.

He was looking forward to a wireless programme, the best of American big bands later that evening. Maybe he'd treat himself to a milk stout or two.

Still smiling, he gathered his papers from his desk, pigeon-holed a couple of letters, and stopping to collect his favourite mug from the mantelpiece, made his way through the waiting room and in to the kitchen.

Now

The station stood empty and abandoned. Once the thriving heart of the community, it had been left to rot. Unused and unwanted, it stood forlorn amid the weeds and brambles, nature reclaiming her own.

The old track still lay in its bed, but the salty air and the exposure to the seasons had badly corroded the metal runners. The boarded-up station buildings stood proud against the elements but any signals, signs or fittings had long since been pilfered by enthusiasts of railwayana.

The two boys traded insults as they raced along the track bed on their bicycles and stopped when they reached the old station.

'They say that place is haunted…' one of them whispered, his eyes wide. 'People won't walk here after dark.

'Rubbish!' scoffed his friend. 'There's no such thing as ghosts! Believe anything you will.

Race you to the bridge.' He took off laughing, cycling as fast as the bumpy terrain would allow. 'Last one home buys the lollies…'

His friend was about to join him when he heard music coming from the old waiting room. Really old music, the sort his Gran would listen to. He waited and listened for a while, mesmerised by the soft dreamy tune. Suddenly, from somewhere inside the station, a door slammed. The boy jumped and looked about him. How could that be? It was a mild day without so much as a breeze. His friend was well ahead, and everywhere was unusually silent. His foot rested on the old track and he became aware of a kind of buzzing, a vibrating through the rail…and then he heard it, some distance away but becoming louder, a chugging sound. The tracks began to rattle. He thought he could smell smoke. And then a whistle, unmistakably a whistle, like one of the old fashioned trains, with the steam powered engines…

The sudden screech of a crow overhead aroused the boy from his stupor. Foot to the pedal he was off like a shot, following his friend into the dim coolness of the woods.

A Note from the author

I hope you enjoyed Little Hubery and the few hours of escapism it afforded you. This book encompasses all of life's little pleasures for me. A light-hearted little book with which to curl up in front of a roaring fire on a cold winter's night, a traditional creepy ghost of a book, but never the stuff of nightmares. Railways, ghosts and the nineteen-thirties, all things dear to my heart. And here I thank the lovely Jackie Statham and her equally lovely daughter Claire of Peak Rail in Matlock, Derbyshire, for allowing me to indulge my passions for both railways and ghosts and for the many happy hours I spent there.

Little Hubery is a work of pure fiction and for the purpose of enjoyment only. So it is here I apolgise to railway experts, thirties buffs and to our wonderful lads and lasses, veterans and those currently serving in the British army, for my crude lack of knowledge thereof. For although I did extensive research in these areas I am, I confess, no expert in any, so please be kind and don't pick holes! Rather enjoy Hubery for the work of fiction that it is.

Enough of my ramblings, for I'm sure you're all curled up and ready to sleep. Please, take Hubery and its message with you into dreamland, but be sure to leave the ghosts behind. Sweet dreams dear reader and remember, there's nothing to fear. After all, none of this is real… or is it?

Jack C. Phillips
2014

Keep reading for an excerpt
from Jack C. Phillips'
latest release

No. 41 Burlington Road

Camelot Publishing 2014

Chapter One

I never went out again after she left. I became a prisoner in my own home. Under house arrest and shackled by my own restraints, I lived a virtual existence which consisted mainly of internet shopping, black and white films and watching the world go by.

Life beyond my door became a soap opera. Something unknown, something to be feared, and fear itself became both my gaoler and my sanctum.

My prison? A bland, ordinary house, on a dull everyday street, in a boring run-of-the-mill town. Burlington Road was built in the nineteen thirties, and apart from the two end houses that were doodle-bugged in forty-four, it survived the war relatively unscathed.

Every house had the same bone structure. A solid but basic thirties design with touches of deco. Obviously there were one or two modern additions, car ports, faux bay windows, storm porches, etc. Our house though, had no such additions. My wife, my soon-to-be *ex*-wife, had a passion for all things thirties and embraced its original features rather than trying to cover them up.

The street itself was in a typical, middle-class suburban area; it was a wide road framed with grass verges and the occasional poplar. Its layout basically consisted of one detached house neighbouring a semi, neighbouring another detached house and so on until the end of the road. It was the same on both sides of the street, and I lived in one of the semis, number forty-one right in the middle, giving me an unrestricted view over most of the street and free reign to speculate over the comings and goings of my neighbours. It's strange how other people's lives take on a new significance when your own was on a back-burner.

I was a writer, of sorts. I wrote jingles and ad campaigns for a local radio station. So it stood to reason that I was a people watcher. I observed and made notes. A voyeur if you like, of mankind and all of its eccentricities and someone equally blessed and cursed with an overly-vivid imagination.

Last night, for instance I dreamed I was in a big house. I knew it was mine, but it wasn't the place I was living in then. The house had four floors and lots of rooms. The fourth floor was a mystery to me. It was dark, dreary and unused and in my dream I had decided to utilise it, to open it up. I came across a door that had been blocked off in the back of a cupboard and went in to investigate. I found a staircase and had barely climbed three steps when I was overcome by the sensation of being watched and such a feeling of evil around me that I turned and ran.

The dream directory told me that the house represented me, my mind, and that the fourth floor was part of my psyche, a part of me that I was afraid of and kept locked away, which when I came to think about it, was actually not far from the truth.

Life was surreal in my little bubble. Time had no significance there. Minutes seemed like hours and hours dragged on for days. My phone had long been disconnected and my letters remained unopened.

I sent text messages to various family members, informing them that I was fine, but needed time alone. So apart from the occasional email from work, the only people I saw then were the man who delivered my groceries, the postman and my neighbours.

The residents of Burlington Road were a fairly mixed bag. Some had lived here for years, like my immediate neighbours at number thirty-nine, Jeremy and Margaret. (Or Victor and Margaret Meldrew as my ex used to call them.) Graham at forty-two, Alan at forty-three and the old dear Clara across at number thirty-eight.

My neighbours were creatures of habit, Victor trimming his hedges every third Sunday of the month, weather permitting and Margaret walking the dogs promptly at eight every morning, whatever the weather. They took regular trips in their caravan, belonged to various clubs and associations and had a fetish for Yorkshire Terriers. Pretension aside, Victor and Margaret were a fairly ordinary couple.

Clara left for bingo on Wednesday afternoons and caught the bus into town every Tuesday to go shopping. She was a colourful character, but had really started slowing down recently. In fact, I hadn't seen her for a couple of days and I wondered had my life still been in full swing, would I have cared? Would I have even noticed?

No. 41 Burlington Road
By
Jack C. Phillips

When his wife suddenly ups and leaves him without warning, Jared Colne is left severely depressed and agoraphobic and cuts himself off from his friends and family. Having no contact with the outside world and dependent upon alcohol and anti-depressants to get him through the day, Jared begins spying on his neighbours on Burlington Road, and soon finds himself living in a dark, fantasy world where nothing is as it seems. As things quickly spiral out of control, Jared realises it's not only his sanity he's in danger of losing.

Who is the pale-faced boy who watches him from beneath the lamp-post across the road? Who lurks in the shadows in the abandoned house opposite? Where does his neighbour Graham go at the dead of night? And who or what is haunting his home, filling his lonely, sleepless nights with fear and dread?

With just the right amounts of comic relief, passion, tears and creepy, tense moments, Burlington Road crosses many genres and is guaranteed to keep you hooked until the story's gripping climax.

Available now in all good bookshops and on Amazon everywhere

Printed in Germany
by Amazon Distribution
GmbH, Leipzig